MAYBE

••

Julia Schultz

Copyright © 2023 by Julia Schultz

All rights reserved.

No portion of this book may be reproduced in any form without written permission from the publisher or author, except as permitted by U.S. copyright law.

Contents

Prologue	1
1. The Annoying Jerk	3
2. B*tch	7
3. Friends?	12
4. "You didn't bring some creature in, did you?"	18
5. Whoa	24
6. His Beating Heart	31
7. Cut Down the Axe	38
8. 10 Years Ago-the Flashback	45
9. Mr. Mirror	51
10. The Rise of the Fever	57
11. Bloody Secrets...	65
12. Driven Away	72

13. Stupid, Unstable Paws	78
14. Like a Madman	84
15. Since Seven	93
16. Sleepover Part 1	100
17. Sleepover Part 2	106
18. Delicious	113
19. Running Back	121
20. Leaving the Pack	127
21. Maybe	134

Prologue

Blood. Everywhere. The cold snow beneath my fingers, the lone little wolf, sniffing my fingers.

It sniffed--she sniffed my fingers and tilted her head. Her grey eyes bore into my green, asking if I was okay. She wasn't the one who bit me.

The huge wolf, the brown one, it was gigantic. It attacked me, wanting me for a meal I guess. But I realized it left me, left me alone with the red wolf. She licked my fingers, and my arm, where the wolf had bit me. My blood finally stops pouring into the snow, and my breathing slows down.

I think I see death coming near me.

For a second I thought she was a regular dog, she was nice and calm. Unlike the other wolf.

But she was different. In her eyes showed kindness, like she could understand my pain.

I'm only seven years old, I'm too young to die this way.

I look at her eyes one last time, grey... grey... grey...And her odd, red fur... red... red...

And soon I only saw black.

I woke up in the hospital room, remembering it all. My head throbbed, the pain shocked me all the way down to my toes. My dad's yelling at the doctors, I could hear him outside the room.

Slowly my eyes close again, and her face fills my mind.

Those humans eyes haunt me till now, ten years later.

The Annoying Jerk

A new student walked into the classroom today, and I could already smell the jerk in him. Yes, the jerk. His hair was fairly fluffy; the light brown nearly reached his eyes—his green eyes. Whispers spread throughout the room, and of course all the girls were freaking out. I had to admit, he didn't look bad. But seriously, if I can smell the jerk in him, there's nothing to look for in him.

He hands a little piece of paper to Ms. Cherri, my language arts teacher. Why would any parent send a kid to a new school in the middle of the semester? I suppose it could be worse. He could've come at the last week of school.

The new boy smiles at the Ms. Cherri, and she told him—or what I think she told him—to find a seat. And just my luck, nobody is sitting by me.

I wouldn't really consider myself popular, but I'm not a nerd either. In popularity, I guess I'm considered middle class. I'm well-liked by everyone. But in this class, there's not a single mind that understands literature. Come to think of it, there's not a single mind that understands anything. It's either I'm smart, or they're really low in their IQ. Or both.

He strolls over, smirking as he comes. I'm already judging him. I judge everyone actually. I know their secrets, their rumors. I can smell their lies. Yes, again, I can smell.

Just putting this out now, I'm a werewolf. I mean, I don't know about vampires and all that, but I can tell you that my species is real. I don't fight any enemies though, since I'm all separated. My father and I live in a house deep inside the woods, so if I change nobody would see me. I'm telling you this now, I love running as a wolf. I love the woods. It's a feeling much better than being human.

The new boy sits next to me, and his smell is so strong. It wasn't a good smell either. I don't know about your opinion on Axe, but it sucks if it's overdone. He leans his head on his hand, and looks straight at me. Being the girl I am, I ignore him.

And he keeps staring.

"Keep staring and you'll won't be able to stare at anything," I said through my teeth.

"Oh, feisty," he mocks. "What can you do little red head?"

I turned to him, and his eyes widened in amusement. "Ha-ha. You don't want to know."

He runs his hand through his brown hair, making it look even fluffier. "I'm so scared." He sees anger in my face. And guess what he did? He widened his grin. "If you really want to do what you said, you might as well do it. Or else you'll be a liar." He winks at me and turns to Ms. Cherri. What did I tell you? JERK.

"Nathan, is there a problem?" Ms. Cherri asks.

He smiles... a really creepy smile... "Everything's mighty fine, Ms. Cherri." Every single head turned to him.

Oh yeah, I forgot to mention, his voice was really deep. Like really, really deep. And I couldn't believe it, most of the girls were squealing in their seats. This is going to be the worst day ever.

Well, if I had anymore classes with him.

My classes pass and so far I haven't had any classes with him. I'm going to my last class now, which was Spanish. And before I even walked in, I could smell him. Ah, darn. I have to start my day with him and end my day with him.

Next to my best friend—April, was the jerk head. He was freaking flirting with her! Dear god! April was twisting her strands of hair within her fingers, going along with it. I'm near clawing the guy, I really am. I didn't know why he made me mad, why he made me so angry, he just did. Just being there, its making me think violently.

April waves at me, and Nathan turns his head. His smile widens. "Hey there, Scarlet," he greets.

"How the heck do you know my name?!" I screeched.

He nods his head over to April. "She told me." Running his hand through his hair, he winks at me. "So... this is some luck, isn't it?"

I rolled my eyes. "Yeah, it's luck all right." There were a few minutes before Ms. Rosa would come in, and I noticed he took my seat next to April. The desks were usually paired up in partners, and the only desk left was with the girl named Ginger and she was always a... uh... moody person. "You're in my seat," I said to Nathan.

"Oh, am I really?" He rolls his eyes at me and continued talking to April. She ignored me, as she would with any situation with a hot guy. I couldn't hold my temper any longer. I sat on him.

"What the heck you are doing?!" he groaned as he struggles to get out of the seat.

"You're in my seat," I repeated, sounding annoyed. "Ah!" I yelled. He was hugging me from behind.

B*tch

Scarlet screams in my lap, and I hold her even tighter. She struggles but she's not strong enough to get out of my grasp. Groaning, she gives me an annoyed look.

I whistled. "Problem, Scarlet?" I beamed my eyes at her and she gives me a death glare.

"Let go of me," she says through her teeth.

Rolling my eyes, I replied, "Make me."

She stops struggling, but instead relaxes against me. Her warmth makes me cozy inside, and I had the urge to actually hug her. Turning her head, her eyes find mine. They were oddly familiar.

I have a phobia of grey eyes... It's weird, I know. But my history of wolves, it's not so great. I remembered that winter day, full of snow, and I got lost in the woods next to my house. A great wolf found me, and attacked me. Even if that red wolf didn't hurt me, her grey eyes haunt me. My father swore he would never let me go into the woods—the wilderness, ever again.

Scarlet stares at me, and her eyes widened just for a second, as if she had remembered something too. Her eyes narrowed, observing me closer. And then something dug into my skin, making me nearly cry out for my life.

She freaking clawed my hands.

"Bitch," I hissed, and I got out of the chair.

She gaped at me, like I had said something wrong. She was being quite a bitch—since first period, anyway. I have to spend the rest of the year with her. Jesus, how much can I take anyway? That girl needed the taste of her own medicine.

Her eyes reddened, and I felt a little sorry for her. She ran out of the classroom, a hand over her mouth, like she was hiding her cry.

"I'm so—," but she was already out the door.

Grabbing a few tissues from the teacher's desk, I wipe away the blood. Yes, she clawed me so hard I was bleeding. Wincing in pain, a hand touches my shoulder. It was April. "You shouldn't call her that," she whispers.

"She fucking clawed me," I reasoned.

"She's..." April couldn't seem to finish her sentence. "She's really sensitive about that word. Scarlet might seem like a... moody person right now, but give her time; she'll be the nicest person you'll ever know." I began to protest but she held up a finger. "Trust me. Scarlet will be your greatest friend if you get to know her." Her eyes look into mine, and I sighed, agreeing.

April smiles and moves her stuff to sit with a blond girl, whom I've noticed never really sat with anybody. She smiles at her though. But... wait... that meant I had to sit with Scarlet.

Ms. Rosa comes in. She was fairly fit, and her brown hair is slightly graying. The bell rings and Scarlet still isn't in yet. I hope I didn't hurt her feelings that much. As if on cue, Scarlet comes in, her eyes still bloody red. She scans the room and sighed dramatically when the only seat left was next to me.

Plopping down in her seat, I could tell she was ignoring me.

"And why are you late, Ms. Perez?" Ms. Rosa asks, and I noticed her accent was more of French.

She shrugs at first but answers politely. "I had a bit of a problem with a student." And it was an honest answer. Nobody seemed to dare say anything—there was complete silence.

"Well, I'll let it pass this time, Scarlet, but please, do be on time." Ms. Rosa's eyes soften, and she began to review greetings and common infinitives for me, since I was catching up. Sadly though, I already knew them all.

I just kept staring at Scarlet, but it was kind of difficult. Her red, wavy hair hid her face. "I'm sorry," I whispered. She didn't reply or budge; she just kept looking at Ms. Rosa. When I touched her arm she flinched, and flashed me another death glare. I saw that she was still crying. "I really am, please forgive me. I don't want to make an enemy on my first day, please," I begged.

Scarlet said nothing. I gave up. I called her one bad word and she gets all emotional about it! Jeez, one bad word!

I tried one more time. "Please."

Her eyes turn to me, lighter and less red this time. And I hear her mutter one word to me, "Burro."

"What?" I asked kind of loudly.

All heads turn to me. Jesus, that's been like this all day. I say something and boom! I'm famous!

"What don't you understand, Mr. Adams?" Ms. Rosa asked, not caring about the attention everyone was giving me. How was I going to get out of this one? "It's quite simple. Surely you've learned the simple hello in Spanish."

I sighed and ran my hand through my hair. "Yes, I have, I just… got confused for a second, that's all," I lied. Everyone whispers thing such as: 'Oh my god', 'He's so slow…' and (one of my favorites) 'I guess only his looks are high, not his IQ.'

And then the bell rang—the last bell.

Everyone got out quickly, especially Scarlet. Her shoulder brushed mine and I just froze in spot. Being the last one out, I had taken quite some time to get to my locker. She was my locker neighbor too. Great.

Note the sarcasm.

The little voice in my head kept repeating April's words though, making me hesitate. Should I be nice to the bitch? Or should I not? The bell rings again and I knew that I was going to be late for my bus. Again.

He called me a bitch. I can't believe he called me a bitch. I mean, I kind of am one… that's why I get so emotional when some people call others bitches. The word isn't set to be used that way. I didn't know why I reacted the way I did anyway.

Sighing, I giggled to myself. He made himself look like a fool in Spanish class. Let's hope he didn't look up the word I called him... Ha-ha, just imagining the look on his face makes me laugh.

I'm on Google Translate right now, trying to remember the word Scarlet had muttered to me. What was it? Burrito? No, I would know what a burrito is. Wait, it was burro.

I typed in 'burro' on my laptop.

I couldn't believe it. She had called me a jackass.

Being friends with this girl is going to be harder than I thought. Well, if what April said was true.

Friends?

I groan as I realized I have school today. It's only Tuesday, but that wasn't exactly the problem. I woke up thinking about him. He was just there... in my bubble of thoughts. Sighing, I walk off to the bathroom and got ready for school.

Okay, this is kind of random, but I love my truck. It's a remodeled 1980 Jeep pickup, rusty red with black leather interior and an epic moon roof on top. Her dashboard is black plastic and her wheel is worn black leather. She runs surprisingly well.

As I walk into school, a lot of people turn to me. What was their problem? But then I realized their stares weren't to me at all, but to the person next to me. I turn my head, and I find myself face to face with Nathan. "Hey," he greets, smiling.

He had little bags under his eyes, but he still had the strength to smile at me. Well, it was better than his smirk. "What...?" Nathan asks.

"You didn't cry all night because I called you a burro, did you?" I asked. He began to answer but I beat him to it. "If I did, I'm sorry."

He looked taken back by my apology. "Not really, I was up all night playing Assassin's Creed 3." My eyebrows furrow in confusion. "It's a video game, sweetie," he says as he pats me lightly on the head. I narrowed my eyes at him, and pinched his hand… but he caught it. "Now, now, I was hoping we can be even today, so no violence," he says like I'm a child.

I walked off to my locker. Hey, it wasn't violent at all, it was just plain rude.

After I was done, I walk Ms. Cherri's room. I notice that over half the class wasn't even here yet, but Nathan was. He was in the same place he was yesterday, and when he saw me at the door, he patted the seat next to him.

I dramatically sit down and found I had nothing to do.

"Really? You don't even want to try to talk to me? I'm hurt." He sighs and slumps down in his seat.

Rolling my eyes, I turn to him. "Why are you such a burro?"

He frowns and looks dead straight at me. "I'm not a burro," he says, stretching the word. "If you actually make an effort to even try to like me, you would find me the total opposite of burro. Sweet—kind, perhaps."

"I really doubt it," was all I said.

"I'll make you a deal," he says and my eyebrows rose. "We try to be friends and if it doesn't work out, then you get to write burro on my forehead in permanent marker, deal?" It sounded like an intriguing idea… I probably will end up writing burro on his forehead anyway…

He gave me his hand and looked at me, asking. "Deal," I confirmed and I shook his hand. Nathan smiles at me as his green eyes... glittered.

The rest of the class—the day, actually—went quite smoothly. I went through all my classes, even eighth period, without the annoying Nathan. Now, I'm not saying he was sweet or anything, it was just nice to know he was making an effort to be friends with me. But there was still something about him that made me uneasy—that made me want to change. It might have been his green eyes and brown hair, reminding me of the woods near my house. He even smelled kind of woodsy... in his little Axe way...

Walking out the school, I see Nathan groaning, clutching his hair and pulling it. "Dammit," I heard him mutter. He probably missed his bus again.

I just stood at the door of the school, behind the little wall, watching Nathan. I sound like a creeper, I know. By the time everyone else left, Nathan was just sitting at the stairs in front of the building, looking at my truck, probably wondering why it was there.

"Do you need a ride?" I whispered from behind him, and he jumps. His eyes showed how pissed off he was, but they also showed sadness. "I can give you a ride in my truck, you know, I wouldn't mind."

"Yes you would," he mutters as he covers his face in his hands, "you wouldn't want to spend time with the new boy, especially if he was a jerk." Where the hell did all of this come from?

"Nathan, what's wrong?" I asked and I sat down next to him. "Did April turn you down or something?" I joked.

He chuckles lightly. "I don't even like her that way." After a moment of hesitation, he adds, "I like someone else."

"Ooooh, who?" Gossip was what I needed right now.

"Oh, a girl," he says, as if it wasn't obvious. Well, he could be gay... I'm not against gay people, for god's sake, I'm a werewolf. "She's spunky... and smart... She has really pretty eyes, but I'm also afraid of them..."

"Afraid of her eyes?" I asked, amused. He shyly nods. "You're some odd little boy."

He remained silent and just looked out, avoiding eye contact. But he wasn't avoiding me at all. It looked as if he were lost in the past—lost in a deep though, and it pained him. His nose wrinkles as he returns back to reality. "So... how about that ride?" He smiles.

"Sure." I got up from sitting on the stairs and pulled him up with me. Together we got in my truck and he sat in the passenger seat, inspecting the truck. "She's nice, isn't she?"

Nathan laughs quietly. "She is quite nice, and comfortable," he says and he wiggles in his seat. He just had to do that, didn't he? "Though she is kind of old."

I frown. "But she's perfect to me, so either you shut up or get out," I threatened. He puts up his hands in surrender, and tells me his address. There was silence for another five minutes or so, but he starts the conversation.

"20 questions?" he suggested.

I laughed under my breath. "So cliché—but why not?" For some odd reason I felt more comfortable around Nathan, like something has been lifted off my chest. "You ask me first."

He ponders, scratching his chin with his finger. "Ah, let's start with something deep. Do you like anybody?"

"Are you, like, a little middle school boy or something? Nobody asks those kinds of questions. And to answer your question, I don't like anybody. There's nobody to like," I shrugged.

He points to himself with widen eyes, as if saying 'Hello?'

"I don't know about you," I said simply. "After all, you seem liked a burro."

"What about now?" he whispers.

"Eh, better," I smile.

We asked each other questions for the next fifteen minutes, and I found out he only lived about ten blocks away from me. Nathan was being generously nice. He wasn't being cocky, or being player. He was simply being a... friend.

When I stopped at the front of his house, I waited for him to get out. Instead, he turns to me holding a poker face. "Can I have a hug?" he asks.

I let out a puff of air, thinking. Should I hug him? Giving up, I open up my arms and he wraps his arms around me, giving me a huge squeeze. It felt nice. "See you tomorrow," he says as he lets go. "Friend."

I smile. "Bye."

And he walked into his house.

Scarlet and I had exchanged numbers and I'm thinking of texting her. Sighing, I plop down in my bed, and close my eyes. But it wouldn't get out of my mind. Her grey eyes, the wolf's grey eyes, I swear, they were really similar. For a second I thought werewolves were actually real. Shaking my head, I threw those thoughts away, thinking about how I'm going to text Scarlet.

"You didn't bring some creature in, did you?"

B eep. Beep. Beep.

Wednesday morning—halfway through the week...

I heard a sound... but I didn't quite know what it was. It was gone the next second; I guess it was the wind or something. I began to walk out of my bedroom, but I heard it again. Turning around, I see nothing that catches my eyes. Not until I heard the noise again.

My phone was vibrating on my nightstand.

I went to my phone, and I what I found was a text from Nathan. Seriously?

Hey, open your door, will you?—NatMan

Say what now?—Scarly

Just... open your door.—NatMan

I'm saying this now, I was a little suspicious. I mean, who tells you to go to open your door in the morning? He sounded like a stalker... or creeper... Not that he isn't already, but still...

Walking down the stairs, I pause on the last step. I could see a little movement through the window near my door. Dear god, is he here? My father would freak out about this... crap. Crap. CRAP. I took a breath and opened the door. He waved at me.

His smile turned from a friendly smile to a pout. "You're wearing that to greet me?" he says, pointing at my Hello Kitty pajamas judgmentally.

I crossed my arms over my chest. "It's six-thirty in the morning, and you want to be dressed up for you?" I whisper, trying not to waking up my dad. "What are you doing here anyway?"

Nathan leans over, looking left to right inside my house. "Why are you whispering?" he whispers.

"My dad," I said simply.

He nods, silently agreeing. And then Nathan's cheeks turn pink and I raised an eyebrow. "I wanted to ride to school with you..." he begins, and I cut him off with a scowl.

"You walked ten blocks just so I can give you a ride? What the hell, Nathan!" I yelled in a whisper. "Who the heck does that?" He reddens even more and gave a little shrug. I rolled my eyes and took a deep breath, trying to keep my temper down. When I look back up to him, I see him smile in amusement. "Did you miss the bus or something?" I ask.

He chuckles. "No... I just wanted to know my friend better."

I grin. "Feeling so determined in the morning already?" He nods.

Nathan runs his hand through his hair, not knowing where to go. He looked so lost... it was kind of funny. He begins to scratch the back of his neck, avoiding my eyes.

"Frootloops?" I ask, trying to ease things up for him. I bit my lip so I wouldn't burst out laughing. He gave me a glare, seeing the laughter in my eyes. "Frosted Flakes, then?" His eyes lighten at my question, and he nods.

Walking into my house, he scans the living room. It was just like any other living room, but it was ancient. And old brown-green carpet was set corner to corner, followed by the bright green walls. Around the room were old paintings, masks, wolf teeth, and even jewelry. Dusty yellow lamps were on each side of the brown, mushy couch. The old love seat had claw marks on the back, from that time I had changed in the house. And the small rectangular table was full of neatly stacked books.

I watch Nathan observe my living room, and his eyes land on a single item that was hung on a wall in the room. It was a small, black glove, from a few years ago. Dad had kept it, so he would know who the boy he had bitten would be. But he never saw him again. He had never changed.

I remember that boy. His blood was all over the perfect white snow. It had felt cold under my paws. I remember him looking at me, and he had quite a dizzy—high look on his face. His eyes had never left mine—those green, forest-colored eyes. When he had closed them, I thought Dad had killed him, that he was dead. But when I heard someone come, their feet breaking into the snow, I ran. And I never saw that boy again.

Quickly, I pull Nathan by the arm into the kitchen, hastily pouring him milk and cereal. Pulling out a chair, I make myself a bowl of Frosted Flakes. We ate in silence. He didn't seem to mind, as he would look out the huge glass doors like I would. The woods—my home, was right in my backyard. Though it's more like... the woods is my backyard.

Nathan would frown, every time he would look out the glass doors. I noticed. He seemed to look down into his bowl, like he was thinking about something.

"Scarlet, you didn't bring some other creature in, did you?" My dad voice breaks into the silence. He walks into the kitchen, stretching. When his eyes found Nathan, both of their eyes widen. "Who's this?" Dad asks. There was a change in his tone.

I swallowed another spoon of cereal. "Dad, this is Nathan. I'm driving him to school today." My father's eyebrows narrowed at Nathan, and then to me.

Scarlet, be careful. I heard him say to me. Nathan looked at us, clearly not understanding the messages my dad is sending me. He's not allowed to know who we are.

I know, dad. He's just a friend.

My father turned to Nathan again. I think it's him, Scarlet. It might actually be him.

I looked at my father as if he was crazy. Him? As in—the boy you bit ten years ago?

Yes.

It can't be, dad. That's impossible.

Nothing is impossible. Just be careful, alright? Don't do anything stupid. And then my father faked a smile at Nathan. "So... Nathan, is it? What's your relationship with my daughter here?" he asks and I shot him a glare.

Nathan looked at me. "Just friends, sir." He looked so... scared...

Dad grins. "Very well," he simply replies. "Scarlet, you better hurry up, there's twenty minutes till school and it's a fifteen-minute drive."

I look at my watch and quickly put my bowl in the sink. Running up the stairs, I quickly change with dark jeans, a pink camisole, and a white hoodie. Finally, I walk down in black Converse and my backpack. My hair was in a neat French braid. I can't believe I did that in four minutes...

Nathan was already at the door, waiting for me. "Bye, dad," I said and I was stopped by his hand on my arm.

"Remember what I said," he reminds, and slowly closes the door behind me.

In the car, Nathan and I stayed in silence. Again. Once in a while I would look at his face, of course when he's not looking. And I couldn't help it, he did look like that little boy. His sharp pale cheeks, those pink thin lips, and those eyes. He looked like the more mature version of that little boy years ago. But a lot of boys have these features.

When Nathan turned around while I was looking at him, he didn't give a cocky smirk like another guy would. He just smiled. But when he smiled, I saw a little faded scar near corner of his right eye. And I just knew that this wasn't just some boy.

Whoa

"What did your dad mean when he said 'some other creature'?" I ask as I get out of her truck. Her eyes widen but they return to normal. "Scarlet?"

"Huh?" She looks at me dumb.

"What did your dad mean when he said 'You didn't bring some other creature in, did you'?" I said again, slowly so she could understand.

Scarlet sighs. "We don't—we don't..." She hesitates. "We can't let strangers in our house." Her shoulders droop and she looks at me.

I didn't know what to say. Well... except... "Why not?"

She shrugs. "It messes up his senses..."

"It what?" I say, bewildered.

She sighs and I could see her breath in the cold air. "I can't explain. His senses just mess up, okay?" I let the subject drop and walk her into the school. "Thanks," she muttered when I open the door. What's up with her? I walk her to her locker, and she didn't seem to mind. Actually, I didn't even know if she knew I was there... I thought she was ignoring me, well, until she once again muttered, "You better get ready for class," she says, avoiding my eyes.

Since I was her locker neighbor, it didn't take me long to open it and get ready. I was finished before her, too. She seemed hesitant to close her locker though, which was quite sad if you ask me. Her mind seemed like it was somewhere else.

I walk next to her to Ms. Cherri's class, but she just looked at her feet. I began to stomp, but she kept ignoring. I snapped my fingers in front of her. Well, that didn't work either. Finally, I made my last attempt to get her attention, which will probably get me killed. I slowly put my arm around her, and then my hand grips her waist lightly. She felt... hot—not that way—but like, she was overheated. But that wasn't the weird thing.

The weird thing was that she didn't kill me at all. She still ignored me. People in the halls were whispering stuff like: 'I thought they hated each other' and 'oh my god, I knew it'. It got quite annoying. Finally, I give her a big squeeze and she looks up at me, surprise of how close I was to her.

"What the—," she began to yell.

But I covered her mouth with my other hand. "What are you thinking about that's so deep? I made every single attempt to get your attention and you continue to ignore me?" I looked straight into her eyes. "Scarlet, what's going on? You've been somewhere else since your dad came into the kitchen. We didn't do anything wrong." She relaxes under my grip but it was more of another sigh. "Tell me." I uncovered her mouth.

"It's none of your business," she whispers. Scarlet pushes me away and walks off to class, leaving me in the hall looking like an idiot.

"And why are you late, Mr. Adams?" Ms. Cherri asks.

I made up some lame excuse. "I was helping a girl pick up her papers," I lied. She nods and continues to hand out some assignment. I walk to my desk and I see Scarlet already scribbling to get the assignment done.

Plopping down in my seat, I began to realize that I kept staring at her. But of course, she doesn't notice. It wasn't like the first day I was here, where she was being a bitch and all that. Come to think of it, I guess April was right. She was pretty cool to hang out with.

Sighing, I began to work on... aw, crap, we have to answer questions about last night's reading. Dammit, I'm already failing my classes. Sneakily, I try to copy Scarlet's answers (but in my own words) and I crossed my fingers. Let's hope she's an overachiever.

When the bell rang, Scarlet was nearly running to the door—though not quick enough. "Please tell me," I said, holding onto her arm. She shrugs off my hold and I could see her wince. A little tear strolled down her face when she looked at me in the eyes. And then she just... walked off.

What the hell did I fucking do now?

My classes went by smoothly, and I sat with my friends at lunch. I didn't see Scarlet at lunch though. Did she leave? I didn't know.

It was finally eighth period, and I was hurt. April was sitting with Scarlet now, leaving me to sit with Ginger. She was more of a bitch than Scarlet... yeah, imagine that. Ms. Rosa made us work with our partners to practice greetings, again, for me. I seriously knew Spanish to the core. It's like my second language! But no, we have to keep reviewing the easy stuff.

Once in a while I would glance over at Scarlet, and she would smile there and then. But I could tell, somehow, that she was faking it. And then I see April patting her shoulder sincerely. I wonder what that was about. At the end of the period, Ms. Rosa finally said I could catch up with the other students by myself. Thank the lord! I thought it would never happen.

And then I felt confused. It was only another minute until the bell was going to ring, but I didn't know how I was going to get home. Should I ride with Scarlet again? Or not? I made the decision to ride the bus and give Scarlet some time alone, whatever her problem was.

When I get on the bus I sat by myself in an empty seat, watching the world go by. It was pretty awesome that Scarlet got to live near the woods, when there's the crowded and polluted city.

I got home in one piece, and I just stood at my stop, still thinking. I was going to make a surprise visit to Scarlet. Again.

I couldn't look at him anymore. His eyes brought back the guilt in me. The blood, the color of his pale face, slowly fading in with the snow, I couldn't think about it.

Though it wasn't me who bit him, it was my dad.

I lay on my bed now, not knowing what to do. I had finished all of my homework, I always finish early. I needed time to think, time to just let it all out.

And what other way to let it all out but to change?

Getting up, I only change into simple shorts and a loose T-Shirt, which was perfect if you're going to change. I walk downstairs and I see my dad in the kitchen, drinking a can of beer and looking out into the woods through the glass doors. "I'm going for a run," I said, opening the glass door.

"Don't injure yourself," he said, and I left barefoot into the woods.

After putting all my school crap in my house, I began walking to Scarlet's house. It wasn't my fault she told me where she lived.

I got so bored I started to kick some rocks, and even cans. Finally, I reach her house. And then it hit me, I did not like the look of her dad's attitude towards me. He seemed fake, like he was warning his daughter. He didn't want me near her, which was probably it. Going on the other side of the house, which I know I shouldn't probably do since this was someone else's property, I see her bouncing red curls and she stalked off into the woods.

And I follow her.

I felt a presence behind me, and once in a while I would turn around. I could smell the slightest smell of Axe, but there was no Nathan here. Well, I didn't see him anyway. Let's hope he didn't follow me, right?

I went to my favorite location to change: Howling Creek. It was quiet and calming, and completely beautiful. Dipping my feet into the water, I shivered. I slowly strip off my shorts, T-Shirt, bra, and underwear, leaving nothing on me. And I change.

I admit, the change was painful at first. Hearing your bones crack and molding into a different shape isn't really something pretty to hear. It was horrifying actually. You see yourself become smaller, but clearer in a way. It was like looking at something over again, but in a different point of view—a different way.

Running, that's what I was doing.

Feeling the wind hit my ears, my thoughts slowly slip away, and I push my paws farther, faster. It was so good to be back in the woods.

Whoa. << This word doesn't even describe how I felt right now.

I followed Scarlet into the woods, and I find her stopping at a little creek, and she walks around it. She smiled to herself, and I could see her relax. It was nice to see her smile again. But I wasn't the one who created that smile. Perhaps she was a wilderness girl.

She dips her toes into the water. Okay, I'm going to go a little off topic about this. How the hell does she walk barefoot into the woods? The branches and twigs didn't even bother her! I was wearing freaking tennis shoes and I still got scratched... Ugh... Anyway, going back to the topic.

When she brings her foot back to the ground, she starts to... uh... take her clothes off. I could see her. She stripped off her shorts, her T-Shirt, leaving her green bra and panties. But she took those off too.

I tried to look away, I swear.

When I finally found the strength to close my eyes, I heard a rustling noise. Opening my eyes again, I couldn't find her. Her clothes lay on the dirt but her body was nowhere to be found. I began to panic.

Correction, I am panicking.

I turned around, going in circles. And I knew it, just then, that I shouldn't have followed. Not only that she was nowhere to be found, but I was lost. I didn't know where to go, and my sense of direction was horrible. Where the hell did she go?

Hearing the rustling noise again, I turn to it. And I turn face to face with something I thought I would never see again.

What I saw in front of me was a pair of grey eyes, and her. The red wolf, she was here, in front of me. And I saw nothing else after that.

When I stopped running, I began to investigate that smell. It took me a few minutes, but I found the source alright.

Nathan really did follow me. Wait, he saw me naked. Fuck. This is some deep shit.

In front of my right now was a pair of green eyes, in shock as I should say. He doesn't say anything, do anything, except stare at me, not believing it. And then, my dear Nathan faints.

He wasn't kidding when he said he said he had a fear of grey eyes.

His Beating Heart

I awoke to a soft hum against my ear, and it felt quite nice. It was a nice tune, the notes went up and down into a soothing melody. But who was humming in my ear? I couldn't quite open my eyes, because I knew if I did I would become blind. Softness was in touch with my fingers, and there was a slight forest-like smell. And I remembered.

I was stalking Scarlet. Jesus, that sounds weird…

Finding the courage to open my eyes, I was stopped by the wetness of my forehead. It wasn't sweat; I wasn't overheated at all. Someone was dabbing my forehead with a wet cloth, I could feel it. And then I open my eyes.

She was looking at me, her head tilted on the side, and a small smile appeared on her face. "Hey there," she said as if she was talking to a child. "What were you thinking, Nathan, following me into the woods?" her perfect eyebrows rose and she crosses her arms over her chest, leaving the wet cloth on my head. I didn't reply. "I'm waiting for an answer," Scarlet says firmly.

"I wanted to talk to you—to know why you were so sad and all that... I thought it was because of me," I explain, hoping she won't kill or yell the crap out of me.

Her eyes soften, but then they narrow. "What exactly did you see?"

Suddenly images of Scarlet in the woods flash through my head, and I wince. She probably already knew the answer, and considering that I'm a guy, she was probably thinking I was some perverted stalker. Seeing my face, Scarlet actually kind of smiles because she knows what I'm thinking about. Her hand finds the cloth but I wince again, thinking that she was about to slap me or something. Yes, I am that afraid of Scarlet right now.

"I'm not going to kill you, Nathan," she says, but then added, "Yet." I gulped in response. "My god, calm yourself. I'm not going to kill you. But you have to promise me something in return." She continues to dab my forehead.

"Promise you what?" I answer, trying to relax.

Her eyes look into mine, and they were quite serious. "You mention this to nobody." She didn't have to continue.

"I promise," I agreed.

There was peaceful quietness and I finally took in my surroundings. It was a bedroom, since I was lying on a bed. A few posters were on the bright green walls, mostly of Ed Sheeran and Christina Perri. There was a black computer desk with a Mac Book Air on it, followed by scattered papers and textbooks. A black bookshelf was stuck into the corner of the room, and it was filled with books, from top to bottom. I look down and I see that the bed was too, also black, and look up to Scarlet.

"You really like black, don't you?" I ask. She nods and walks out of the room with the cloth. When she returned I asked her, "How come not the couch, but in your bedroom? You know, if you really wanted to sleep with me, you could've just asked."

She snorted, "Yeah, I would so sleep with you, virgin." How the hell did she know? When she looked at my face, her snort turned into a laugh. "I'm right, aren't I?" She said between her laughs. After she was done, she said, "And to answer your question... I told you, strangers mess up my dad's senses. You don't need to know why," she put her hand up to silence me. When she put it down, she smiled, "Now tell me why you fainted in the middle of the woods."

Her eyes flash in my mind. "There was a wolf."

"So?" Scarlet shrugs, "There are lots of wolves."

I whispered, "It had grey eyes..."

Scarlet made a gesture for me to scoot over, and so I scooted over on the bed. She lay down with me, one of her hands supporting the back of her head. Staring up at the ceiling, she says, "You didn't faint when you saw me, and I have grey eyes. Maybe you have a phobia of wolves."

"But I'm not afraid of dogs though," I pointed out. She shrugs. "I had some bad history with wolves though."

"Yeah? Well, what happened?" Scarlet asks, her voice beginning to crack.

Ignoring the pain on my shoulders, I turn to her, leaving my weight on one arm. "It all began when I was seven."

"Seven?" She sounded like she was on the verge of crying.

"Yeah," I sigh. "My dad had taken me to go hunting with him, since there was nobody to take care of me. My mom was at work, all the way in Canada, not here in Mississippi. Anyway, I was a boy, and my curiosity overruled my common sense. I had a horrible sense of direction, and I still do now," I smiled, but then it faded. "So basically, I got lost in the woods in the freaking winter. I almost froze to death in that cold snow. But then I saw a brown wolf, and it was huge. It tackled me into the snow, and that didn't really help the fall. I couldn't breathe and I felt my head, burning. And I knew the wolf had scratched me. Its teeth bared in front me, and the growling that came out of it scared the crap out of me." I let out a long breath. "And then it bit me in the arm, and my god that was painful. When I opened my eyes, I saw this little wolf, she had red fur, much like the color of your hair, Scarlet." She winced and I could see her silently crying, though I continued. "She helped me feel better. She licked my bloody hands, my arm, and little bit of my face. I saw her grey eyes, and they were so beautiful, yet so human. The snow suddenly didn't feel so cold—so useless. I blacked out though, and woke up in the hospital." I plop back down on the bed, my arm was sore. "That was basically it. I don't know what my phobia is, I guess. It's either grey eyes, or wolves. Maybe even grey-eyed wolves. Who knows, right?"

I felt her move next to me, and I see that she had flipped around and buried her face into one of her pillows, crying. I knew it was a sad story, but I didn't know that it was that sad. I flipped over on my stomach too, and I hugged her. Slowly I felt her arm go around my torso, and she squeezed me as hard as she could. And she cried into my shoulder.

Hearing his story, I couldn't help but cry. The pain he went though, and all at the age of seven. It's not really surprising that my eyes haunt him, I was the last thing he saw before the hospital. Never had I felt this sad before. All this guilt is finally pouring out of me, like everything that was bottled up has finally been lifted.

I bury my face into his shoulder, and for every sob I get a gulp of his smell of Axe. His smell now though, instead of being annoying, is now actually comforting. He's stroking my back, calming me down. I didn't even care about the incident in the forest just an hour ago, I was just sad about the fact that I will haunt him forever.

When I calmed down, I took my face away from his shoulder. He had my tear stains on his T-Shirt. You could see this big glob, it looked like he's sweating...

"You okay?" He asks, his eyes full of concern. "It really wasn't that sad, was it?"

I wiped my tears with the back of my hand. "It really was, and it really is." There was silence.

"Are you a werewolf?" he asks suddenly, and I stiffen.

"What?" I said kind of loudly.

He shook his head. "Never mind, it's nothing. I had a weird thing going in my head. For a second I thought you were actually a werewolf, that's all." He shrugs.

"Why would you think that?" I ask, curious.

"Well, that wolf's grey eyes were kind of similar to yours, for one. And you stripped your clothes off in the middle of woods," I slapped him, "Ow! That hurts." He pouts. "And then you disappeared really fast, leaving your clothes behind. So maybe you were going to change or something. I read too much." He sighs.

I chuckle, "Yeah, you do."

We breathe in the silence, and I felt relaxed—relieved. I was so relieved that the boy that my dad bit was still here, still alive. But he didn't change, he didn't believe in werewolves. He is one. Well, he's supposed to be one. I wonder what had happen, and why he didn't change.

"I can get used to this," Nathan says, interrupting my thoughts.

"Get used to what?"

"Hugging you, in bed," he replies.

I jumped as I realize we were still intertwined with each other, from me crying. I started to scramble away but Nathan held me close, not letting me go. "Now, now, don't ruin the moment," he mumbles into my hair. And I gave up, although I could so have pinched him away. It felt nice to hear his heart beating against my ear. I sigh and I could feel his smile, and he squeezes me tighter.

"You're really warm," I said, and my cheeks warmed for saying it.

"Thank you," he says. "But I prefer the term hot over warm." Nathan chuckles to himself. Hey, it's not me who ruined the moment here. "I can't believe you stripped off your clothes in the middle of the woods," he says, testing me.

"I'm glad you enjoyed it," I said sarcastically.

"I didn't really hate it, now did I," he replies. I slapped him again. "Ow!"

I smile to myself and before I knew it I fell asleep into his arms.

Cut Down the Axe

I was awakening by the warmth that began to touch my face. It was the sun; I could see the orange through my eyelids. I groaned and hugged my pillow tighter. But there was a problem; I didn't have a hugging pillow. There was hot fire burning against the tips of my fingers. It felt rigid and smooth at the same time. I began to wonder, with my eyes closed, what the heck I was touching. As I open my eyes, I regret it so much. The light, it burned.

When my vision focused, I found out I was really intertwined with… Nathan? What the heck! His arms were wrapped around my torso and I the same, though my hand was touching his… uh… abs. My leg was wrapped around both of his and he's breathing into my hair. I'm a freaking monster when I sleep. I slowly took my leg and arm off of him. The only problem was his arm around my torso. Now how do I get out of this?

I slowly touched his hand, hoping that I wouldn't wake him, and began picking it up, moving it away from my torso. But then his hand slaps back down, and I cry for a second of pain. And then he moaned softly into my hair, hugging me tighter. This task is going to be impossible. Giving up, I push his chest away from me, but he hugs me even tighter. What the heck?

"Nathan," I groaned, "Get off of me!"

I could hear the deep, ruffle sound in his chest. Why the heck was he laughing? "Ah, that was fun," he says, beginning to sit up on the bed and I the same. As I began to push my messy, red hair away from my face, I heard Nathan say, "That was hilarious. You suck at not waking up someone by the way," he added later.

I turn to him with wide eyes. "You were faking being asleep the whole, freaking time?!"

His hand goes to the back of his neck. He looked kind of nervous... "Well, uh, maybe I was?" His forest eyes look into my grey, asking for a reaction. He was probably expecting something like yelling, screaming, or especially violence. "Scarly?" he said, his cheeks turning a little pink.

I cross my arms over my chest. "Don't call me that. You don't deserve to call me that." I frown. As I got up from my bed, I walk out the door, and I could smell the cheesy potatoes and if I'm correct... steak. My nostrils filled with heaven but not until the smell of Axe filled too. It wasn't a really good smell.

"Whoa," I heard Nathan say.

"I know," I smiled. I walk down that stairs without him, and into the kitchen.

Everything was already set up, plates, silverware, everything. My dad took off his apron, and turned around, facing me. He gave a small smile but it turned into a slight frown. I already knew what it was, nobody had to tell me anything. Anyone would recognize the person from a mile away. Nathan seriously needed to cut down the Axe.

"Hi, Mr. Perez," Nathan greeted as he neared me.

My dad forced a smile. "Hello, Nathan," he says. "Would you mind staying over for dinner?"

Nathan grinned, "I'd love to, sir." I've never seen Nathan this polite before. I mean, he was always the talkative one in the classroom. Teachers didn't like him very much. It's weird though. He gets A's and all that. Nathan's pretty smart, well, most of the time.

"Wonderful," my dad says, kind of through his teeth. Nathan didn't seem to notice and sat down at our dining table. Our kitchen and dining room were kind of merged together.

We chewed our way through dinner, Nathan complimenting my dad's cooking once in a while. My dad and I remained quiet throughout, and thank the lord it wasn't awkward silence. We would look at each other, sending each other our messages, and Nathan would look at the both of us, and then shrug it off. Sometimes I feel bad for that clueless boy.

Dad, it's him. He's the boy. I said urgently.

I know, Scar. I heard. Dad continued to eat as if it was nothing.

But dad, it was him! He was only seven! You need to find out why he hasn't changed!

Why do I need to find out?! His voice roar in my head and I wince.

He didn't change. He's not like one of us. But what had stopped him? Why did it stop? Why didn't he complete the change? I rushed all the questions in my mind that I could think of. Why didn't he change? I whispered. Why, dad?

I don't know. I heard my dad say. When I looked up from my food I saw that his eyes had reddened. God knows what I did to this boy. I thought he was dead, Scar. And now he's right here, in front of me—in my kitchen. To see that he hadn't change, that I had only caused his childhood to be a nightmare, it not only hurts him, it hurts me. I would never do that to him intentionally.

Why did you bite him?

You know why, Scar.

And with that, my father stood up to put his plate in the kitchen. He stood at the glass doors. "I'm going for a walk," he says, and slowly he disappeared into the woods. I had never seen my dad so down, well, I have seen him worse. When he had bit Nathan, and saw the bloody snow, and not Nathan's body, it wrecked him. He had cried himself to sleep, in the house that we used to live in. Dad would stare into the crackling fire in the living room, hugging his knees. He thought Nathan was dead, and I did too. But over the years, I tried not to think about it, that that boy was somewhere better now. But now he was somewhere better. He was on this living earth, with me.

Nathan snaps his fingers in front of me. "What're you thinking about?" He smiles and eats his last slice of potato. I felt my cheeks warm and my eyes water. "You're not going to cry again, are you?" he asks after seeing my face. It sounded like he had actually cared.

"No, I'm fine," my voice cracked.

He shrugs. "Whatever. You can always have my shoulder to cry on," he winks. Nathan stands and pushes up his sleeves, then grabs the plates. "I'll wash them."

"Okay, thanks." I took a sip of water.

He stopped midway of his walk to the sink and turned around. "Most people would stop their guest from washing the dishes and wash them themselves."

I grinned. "I'm not most people." He shakes his head with a little laugh, and washes the plates.

Nathan stood at my door, and turns to say goodbye. "Bye, Scarlet. See you tomorrow, 'k?" he tilts his head to the side and pinches one of my cheeks. I stuck out my tongue at him and he laughs.

"Want me to drive you home?" I ask calmly.

He shakes his head. "Nah, I think I'm good for a few blocks."

"At least let me walk you home," I pleaded.

He raises an eyebrow. "Does someone care for Nathan's safety?" I nod like a child. "I'm not making you walk twenty blocks for me, Scarlet. Then no one would walk you home." Nathan crosses his arms. He really thinks he's going to win this argument.

"I think I can take care of myself, Nathan," I sigh. He begins to protest but I cut him off. "Let's make a deal. We'll arm wrestle. If I win, I get to walk you home. If you win, well, then you have a chance of dying by walking home alone at night. Deal?"

Nathan laughs. Again. "You think you can beat these?" he asks, showing me his biceps. Yes, they were very muscled. But I'm a werewolf, am I not? I think I can handle a seventeen year old boy. I nod as my answer to his question. He cracks a grin and gestures the coffee table in my living room. He has his arm ready and I walk and kneel on the soft carpet, gripping his hand. And we wrestle.

We were neck to neck. Both of us were still at the same spot we started with.

"Damn, Scarlet, how are you so strong?" Nathan says, nearly losing his grip with the sweat of his hand.

I chuckle. "How are you so weak?" I ask, and he gives me a glare. I hold on for a few more minutes, and slowly Nathan begins to weaken. I could see his hand, slowly going down... down... down... and after seven minutes of sweaty hands, I won. Yeah, I was so surprised that I had won.

The expression on Nathan's face was hilarious. His eyes were wide and his jaw nearly hit the floor (not literally, but you know).

"I want a rematch," he whines minutes later after shock.

"A deal is a deal," I said with a mother tone.

"But I never made the deal!" he says.

And I pause halfway out the door. He didn't. He didn't agree to the deal. "Too bad, Nathan," I gave in. "I'm walking you home."

He sighs. "Why do you even care?" he whispers.

I was near pulling out my hair with this kid. "Because if I don't walk you home, something out there will probably fucking eat you alive, and there would be nobody to annoy me. Happy?" He smiles and begins to say something until I interrupted him, "Good. Now let's go.

There were a few minutes of silence until Nathan stopped it. "Does your father not like me?" he asks.

My hands were inside the pockets of my hoodie, and now I'm fiddling. "No, you just remind him of the past."

"The past?" He seemed surprised. "What happened in his past?" Nathan's eyes turn to me.

"None of your business," I mumbled. "I do know something he doesn't like about you though," I added, trying to get him off the topic. He didn't seem to care and didn't push me for an answer.

"And what is that?" Nathan said it like he knew there was nothing about him to dislike. Psh, like that was true.

"Your overload of Axe. It's disgusting," I pinched my nose dramatically.

He stuck his tongue out at me, "is not."

"Cut down on the Axe, Adams," I said with a smile. I'm beginning to like annoying him. This, my friends, is called payback.

We walked to his house with a couple of weird topics of conversation, but I didn't seem to mind. Nathan was really easy to talk to, and he wasn't such a bad guy either. It's hard to imagine that he was the little boy that was lying in the snow ten years ago.

10 Years Ago-the Flashback

It pained me whenever I went into the woods. The smell of blood was always on my lips, the tip of my tongue. That little boy's body would flash in my mind. He looked crippled—abandoned. As I walk into the woods now, all I could do was see that boy now—Nathan, smiling kindly at me. He didn't know who I am, what I did to him.

I never thought that there would be a pain greater than the death of my pack, but there is. I wouldn't say that guilt would overrule the love of your family, but this—this was cruel. Seeing something you have regretted come back, it's like a haunting nightmare.

Closing my eyes, I blindly move my fingers to the nearest branch, holding onto it. I take a breath and slowly, I change into the monster I was ten years ago.

Ten years ago, I was up in Canada, not Mississippi. It was cold, though my pack and I loved it. We loved the snow beneath our paws. But when came fall, there was a wild fire. Being a werewolf, your senses are slightly weaker than a real wolf's. Though, for some reason, the fire wasn't sensed by anyone until it hit our area. It came—the fire, quicker than any fire I've ever seen before. And the worst was that everyone was in different areas of the woods.

Run! I told everyone.

I was seconds late. The fire reached the river, and I couldn't believe it. The river too was on fire. I ran—I ran for my life, my wife behind me. Well, that was what I had thought. I heard the sound of ruffled leaves, though it stopped. I turned around to see my wife, burning before my eyes.

Go Darrin, go. Her faint voice said in my head. Leave.

And she vanished within the fire.

I ran in all directions, looking for a way out. Trees fell, making it even more difficult. It was like a maze in hell, complicated, dangerous, and hot. I got burns multiple times on my back. My paws were on fire by the ground below me.

When it felt as if I had been running for hours, I collapsed. I was out of the woods and I changed back quickly into a human, and walked onto the empty highway. My clothes were burned in the cabin I had in the woods. I was sure of it. So I walked with pain along the ground of the highway, hiding behind the trees, and waiting for red flames to disappear.

My home burned for another hour.

And I had reached the city.

I turned back into a wolf; my human feet were sore. When I changed however, I smelled something familiar. I followed it, and I saw her, my only one left. Scarlet, as small as she was, had followed me.

I licked her tiny wolf head, so small and so fragile. On her paw was a faint wound, healing itself. Scar, I said, Are you alright?

Yes, papa, I heard her say as she nuzzles into my fur.

All I could do that day was cry. We had found a close family of ours who had given us a temporary home, though till today they're wondering why neither of us had clothes on in the woods. We claimed that we were going for swim. But I didn't cry for the embarrassment. I cried because my family had die, my home was gone. My only family left was Scarlet, and she was so young. She didn't know a thing. All she wanted was her mom. And to be honest, I kind of wanted her mom too.

That night I ran off, leaving her behind. I didn't know where I was going, and I didn't give a fuck. Life was unfair, even as a free wolf. I walked as a wolf until the sun rose—I walked in the ashes of my home. It began to snow, even in the fall. But hey, it was Canada. Slowly the dirt became snow, and my pace slowed down.

I turn around to see Scarlet, her head tilted to the side. Where are you going? She asks.

I was so ashamed. I was so ashamed to leave my own family behind. So, in the spurt of the moment, I wanted to create a new pack, a new life. My paws just ran without me, into the deep white snow.

Papa! Where are you going?! I hear Scarlet say, following me behind.

Suddenly this boy came into my hearing. He was holding a toy within his gloves, but it was a little shovel. He was laughing to himself, and it was like music to my ears, that laughter. Though he was alone, looked alone; I just wanted to make him... happy. I neared him, making it obvious that I was behind the bushes, and he came.

"You're a dog!" he exclaimed and petted my head. I liked his gloves. "You're cute! Do you have a name?" he drops the shovel and starts to pet me with both of his hands.

And I tore him with my teeth. His jacket ripped easily, and within seconds the blood fills me mouth. I bite him. I bit him. But I didn't hear his scream. It was my daughter's scream; she had screamed for him. The boy lay unconscious in the snow below me, and I shook my head. What had I just done?   I sniff his hand, and I put my ear near his chest. He was still breathing, but it was growing slower. You killed him, the voice in my head said. You murdered a boy.

Being the coward that I was, I ran away.

I never saw him again.

That night I sat near the fire, hearing it crack within the night. I hugged my knees, staring into it. But all I could see was that innocent boy taking all the pain I was giving him. I had only wanted a family. Was that so much to ask? Slowly I cried. Warms tears caressed down my cheeks.

Scarlet said that it was alright. She said that the humans had found him and taken him away to a better place. But who knew that the world was this small?

Now, seeing him the way he is now... I can't help but wonder what had happened. I had ruined his childhood. What kind of a person am I? Oh wait; I'm only half of one. It was selfish of me, to start over with a selfish boy.

As I see his face appear in my head again, I run faster, his blood in my mouth beginning to get stronger. And slowly, though more of quickly, I run back.

I woke up with sweat dripping off of my forehead. Why? I just had a recap of my childhood.

Seeing those grey eyes today must've given me the scares again. That was probably it. I don't know. All I saw was the blood on my hands, my arms, the painful feeling, though it was just the numbness that overcame it. I shook off the feelings of my dream and walk off to the kitchen.

My plan was to get a glass of milk, but things don't always go out the way you plan. Instead of getting a glass of milk, I decided to make my famous tuna salad. It took fifteen minutes of my life, though the five minutes of heaven made up for it. After that I brushed my teeth again, climbed into bed and hoped that I won't have any more childhood flashbacks.

But you see, my phone buzzed.

I reached for my phone on my nightstand and unlocked it, trying to see through my blind eyes. It was a text for Scarlet, though I don't see why she would text at this hour.

He doesn't know he's one of us, April. What do I do? Nate should've changed.—Scarly

I stared blankly at the text that was clearly meant for April. What did she mean I should've changed?

Though, being the person I am, I couldn't help but have this little feeling of joy in my heart that Scarlet actually talks about me to April. Jeez, I sound like a girl right now...

I replied to her.

Wrong person, ttyt though—NatMan

Mr. Mirror

I woke up feeling slightly hyper. And guess what? My father is making pancakes. Yeah, that's what I need, more sugar to spice up my day. Or should I say... sweeten. Oh god, what is happening to me?

Oh yeah, did I forget to mention? You have to face Nathan today. My eyes widen in the mirror as my mind speaks to me. Crap! I totally forgot! I spit out the foam in my mouth and rinse, hoping so dearly that I could think of a backup plan for today.

Of course I'm going to avoid him; that's the only way to not interact with him. Well, if I did have a conversation, I wonder what he would say... It would probably go like this...

Hey Scarlet, I didn't know you talk about me with your friends...

I don't!

Oh? Then what was that text about?

It was nothing! An accident!

An accident, I can believe. But the fact that it was about me... that's kind of rude, Scar. Didn't your parents teach you not to talk about others behind their backs?

I wasn't... I didn't...

You know, I could totally see that whole conversation play in real life.

Getting annoyed, I change into a pair of dark jeans and an orange striped shirt. I walk down the stairs and into the kitchen, where my dad was flipping his famous blueberry pancakes. And believe me, they were fucking delicious. (Excuse my "French".) If you haven't tasted my dad's pancakes, you don't know what heaven is.

"Morning, Scar," my dad said as I walked into the kitchen, and he handed me a plate of three. He knew me too well. "Why are you sweating?" he asks, touching my forehand with his finger, then wiping it on the apron he was wearing.

I wiped my forehead to see that it was full of sweat. EW... Why was I so worked up about this? I used the back of my sleeve to wipe off the remaining sweat (gross, I know) and smiled at my father. "I took a shower?" I said, more a question than a statement.

"Well, you stink," he said, taking an amused sniff.

While taking my plate over to the table I take a little sniff at my underarms, wondering if he was really kidding. I mean, I'm clean and all... I was just checking.

When I finished eating my heaven of a good breakfast, I drove myself to school in my awesome truck. However, I couldn't help but think of what Nathan will say when I get to school. Forget what he'll say, what will I say? Ugh, why didn't I check who I was texting? You're really stupid, Scar, my unhelpful conscience says. Yeah, no dip, Sherlock. Being literally one red light away from school, I seriously thought about skipping. This is just plain scary.

Who knew the boy that dad bit will move to the same area as us?

It's a small world after all.

Why are you quoting one of your least favorite songs? I'm going crazy. I can't stay on topic with anything.

I pull into the parking lot, grabbing my backpack and head up to my locker. Let's just say, it's hard to avoid the person you're avoiding when he's your locker neighbor. Plus, if you also have first period with that person... that doesn't help either.

Just when I got to my locker, I looked around cautiously for him. Though I guess my wolf sense of smell was stronger than its sight. "Hey, Scarlet," Nathan said, putting in the combination for his lock. "I need to talk to you." I stayed quiet, hoping he wouldn't notice. "I know you can hear me," he says, and I sensed him staring at me while I was still putting my books in. I slammed my locker when I was done, practically running away. Well, until he grabbed me by the arm. "And where do you think you're going?" he asks.

I gulped. "I'm going to class," I said calmly, and stopped struggling in his grip.

"I need to talk to you," Nathan stared into my eyes. "Plus, we have ten minutes." He lets go of me and shut his locker and leaned on it. Now he's intently watching me. And being the person I am,

I squirmed under his stare. "So, what do you mean I should've changed?"

"I don't know what you're talking about," I said a little too quickly.

I thought he was going to give me one of his usual smirks, but instead he frowned, and well, vulnerable. "I know you're lying…" he says. "And what do you mean 'he doesn't know he's one of us'? Are you implying that I'm a girl behind my back?"

At that, my lips turn into a small smile. "I wasn't implying anything. Though…"

His eyebrows shot up, "Though?"

I grinned. "Though you do look at yourself in the mirror longer than the average girl…" I put a finger to my chin, making it look like I was thinking.

"How do you know about my time at the mir—," and he stopped himself. I couldn't help it. I burst out laughing. People walked by our lockers, having questionable looks on their faces. That just made me laughed even more. "You really suck, you know that?" he says, beginning to drag me to first period.

"You—are—so—stupid," I giggled.

"Yeah, yeah. You had your fun. Now answer my questions, will you?" Now that made me stopped laughing.

I tried on my new-and-somewhat-improved-over-the-years poker face. "You're one of the evil queens in fairytales."

"Okay, see, that wasn't so hard to answer, was it?" he said, and then stopped walking. "Wait, what did you just say?"

That made me laughed. Again. For five minutes.

Let's just say my face was as red as a tomato from trying to control my laughter.

No seriously, tears were in my eyes.

And it wasn't even that funny.

"Stop laughing, will ya?" he mumbles. "It wasn't even that funny."

"It wasn't to you, Mr. Mirror," I said evilly. Nathan banged his head straight down to the table. I heard whispers starting to get louder and looks were given to him as if he were crazy. "You're going to start calling me that now, right?" he asks.

I pat his back. "It's okay. Your beloved mirror won't make fun of you," I grinned and he just groaned through his arms.

"You still haven't told me the actual answers," he points out ten minutes later into class.

"And I never will," I said simply.

"But if it's about me, I think I should know," Nathan says, and I didn't hear any part of his voice that said that he thought any of this was funny. In fact, when I looked up to him, he was paying attention to the assignment, but his lips were in a frown, and his forest green eyes got a little darker.

I sighed. "It's more like I can't tell you," I whispered.

Nathan turns to me. "Why not?"

"I can't tell you that either."

"Well... you have to tell me something," he whispers as he writes another answer on his worksheet.

"Hey, Nathan," I called, and he hummed in return. "How's Mrs. Mirror doing?" And he literally leaned back in his chair and slid down under the table to finish his worksheet. He got quite a few looks...

The Rise of the Fever

Shit. I really need to learn how to control myself. I had finally lost it. And if you're wondering what in hell's world it is, it's my sanity. I have gone insane, everyone! Yeah! Yeah... no.

Let me fill you in on what has happened within the past month.

School went regularly; Nathan was nearly failing all of his classes, all except Spanish, he's actually smart in that. It's funny though, he didn't what burro was, and Spanish was like his second language. Eh, sucks for him, I'm better.

Each day went in the following order: [1] We go to school. [2] We have our classes. [3] We go home.

The schedule seems so simple, right? Nothing can happen. Ah, but there is number four. It's really surprising to me that I could actually get along with Nathan, well, most of the time. After we went home, I would do my homework, being a good student. But, after that, I would hang out with Nathan. This didn't happen everyday, just often. But any day I don't spend my leftover time with him feels empty, boring.

Dad kept pressing me on asking him about what had happen after the wolf attack, if he had any odd conditions or anything. I felt uncomfortable though, every time I tried to ask. I didn't want to dwell on the past when he was alive. That was all I cared for, his life. I was just happy he was goddamn breathing.

It did interest me. How come he didn't turn into a wolf? I laugh every time I think of this, since he's afraid of wolves. Well, more of my dad and I...

Nathan didn't ask about the accidental text, he had finally let it go and I was relieved.

And then came the night of the storm, which was two days ago.

It was a sunny evening, and dad was washing the dishes. Nathan had came over for dinner. Till this day, after all those times he came over for dinner, dad was still uncomfortable with Nathan's scent in the house, bringing him back memories.

"Can we..." Nathan began, though his voice was shaky. "Can we go into the woods today? Instead of hanging out in your room?" I could see dad holding a plate that laid still in the running water.

"Y-yeah, sure," I answered as shaky as him.

I opened the glass door and he walked through. When I was about to close the door, dad stopped it. "Careful," he whispered, and I nodded. Then I went off after Nathan.

"So," I said as I caught up with him, "Why the change?"

He looked down at his feet, not looking at me. "Change is good."

"Not always," I argued, and when I looked at him there was a small smirk on his face.

We walked in silence after that. I didn't know where I was going, and I really doubt he knew, since he's never been in the woods here. After a few more minutes though, I noticed we were going towards Howling Creek. My cheeks warmed when I thought about Nathan seeing me... you know. Sadly, Nathan noticed my pink cheeks and chuckled, remembering too.

When we neared the creek, he just sat down next to it, touching the water with his fingers. There was a small smile on his face as he looked down into the water. I sat next to him--across from him, and I stared at our reflections.

Of all places in the world, the boy my dad nearly killed is right here. I can't help but think, is this fate or is this revenge? Is God punishing me for what my dad had done, making me see him everyday? Or is he giving me a chance to fix what my father had done? Or... maybe it's just a small world.

I stared dreamily at the water, that is, until I saw Nathan staring at me.

"Scarlet," he said, his voice cracking. "What are you?"

My heart had stopped right then, but I didn't give up on my cover. I wasn't going to blow this up. "What do you mean?"

"What are you? Besides human and insane," he asked, half joking. I looked into his forest green eyes, and I nearly drowned inside. Why couldn't I tell him? What was I protecting him from?

This is the easiest question ever, the voice in my mind said. Your dad nearly killed him. Do you really want him to know that? Damn.

"I don't get your question, Nathan. I mean, what are you?" I asked back.

"Tell me something, Scarlet," he said seriously, and my heart beated rapidly waiting. "Why were you here, stripping your clothes off? Where did you go?" Nathan looked so serious, I couldn't joke this out. I couldn't nag.

"Where did you think I went?" I questioned. Why was he bringing this up all of a sudden?

"I'm asking for a reason, Scarlet," Nathan rolled his eyes. Though he was quiet, I could tell that he was serious and that he was still looking for a reason.

I swallowed the guilt in my throat, and shakily said, "What do you think I am?" It was such a small whisper, such a simple question. I was probably blowing my cover already. He saw the glove in my living room, he saw me change. It was so obvious. Did he really need me to spell it out?

Nathan looked into my eyes and I noticed that his eyes had darkened. He licked his dry lips and frowned. "I think... that if I told you what I think you are... you'll think I'm the insane one."

A gasp escaped my lips. "You are," I joked, trying to keep cool. "Nathan?" I said, and he hummed, looking at me. "What happened, if you remember, at the hospital after you were bitten?"

Nathan nodded at me, looking at the dirt and playing with the grass around him, avoiding me. Soon though, he answered. "I kinda blacked out after I saw the little red wolf... but I could hear bits of things happening when I was still concious. My dad was yelling at the doctors, nurses. And the pain in my arm was throbbing. When they finally put me to sleep though, I woke up hearing that there was something odd in my arm that the wolf had probably given me. They didn't know if it was bad or not, if it would kill me or not. A few weeks after that, they let me go. They never found out what it was." He shrugs and touched the water again.

The blood is still in him, probably, the voice in my head thought. I let out a sigh. I owe you so much, Nathan. I'm so sorry you're like this.

"Do you--do you..." I tried to phrase my question so it would make sense to him. "Do you ever feel like you're trapped in your own body, but you don't know how to get out?"

He stared at me. His eyes were calm but they gave no emotion. What was he thinking? "Sometimes, I just want to... run away. But I have to control myself... I do feel trapped. Though I think everyone feels like that once in a while."

There's still hope... there has to be.

I didn't know that the sky had darkened, well, not until the sound of thunder echoed my ears. "We should probably get going," I said, and he nodded in agreement.

We both got up, brushing the dirt on our pants, and started walking home. Soon though, there was rain. I knew it wasn't safe to run home, but it was safer than staying in the rain. The ground had become muddy, sticky. It would be so easier if I was a wolf.

It was hard to tell if I was going to slip on the mud on my human feet, or get stuck in it. I love the rain and all, but running in it was feeling ridiculous.

We made it back to my house, and we left out muddy shoes outside so they could dry later. Dad rushed us in, giving us towels to dry ourselves. I took a shower and changed into my PJs while Nathan sat in the living room. During my shower though, there was a blackout. Imagine showering in the dark. Scary, isn't it? Luckily, I knew where everything was, thanks to my wolf senses.

I came down stairs into the living room, with guy clothes in my hands. "Here," I said, tossing the clothes to Nathan. He caught the jeans and T-shirt, looking at them.

"Why do you have guy clothes?" he asks, smirking.

"They're my brother's," I answered.

His brows furrowed. "You have a brother?"

I looked at Nathan, and a million pictures flashed through my mind. The fire, my family, my old home. Everything was up in flames. And all I could say was, "I had one."

Nathan's eyes soften. "I'm sorry."

"It's alright, just go change," I said. He left and I grabbed a blanket on the couch, wrapping it around myself. The fire place made it bright and warm in the living room, its flames beautifying the darkness.

Tears threatened to fall out of my eyes. Every time I saw red flames, all I saw was my running family, dying within my innocent home. I stare into the fire in front of me, thinking. It was because of that cursed fire that caused Nathan to be like this. Soon my vision blurred, and I felt an arm around my shoulders.

"Why are you crying?" Nathan said softly. "Scarlet?" he called, pulling me closer.

His scent filled my stuffy nose, but all I could taste was the blood in my mouth, his blood. My heart hurts so much. It pained me to see him comforting me, when I should be comforting him. He was nearly sacrifice to be my family, my second one. I didn't deserve this, and neither should he.

"What's wrong?" He asked again, tugging. "You can trust me."

You'll run away, Nathan. But isn't that what I want? Him to not be near me? I couldn't think straight.

"I'm sorry," I whispered as I shivered.

"What are you sorry f--," he stopped mid-sentence.

I hungrily press my lips against his, hands carefully on the side of his head. My fingers found their way to his soft, dark hair. He kissed me with the same amount of force and our lips moved in unison. I didn't know if I felt happy or sad.

His hands had a firm grip on my shoulders; his touch was so warm against my skin. It burned.

And then I tasted blood in my mouth, and hell it wasn't my blood. It was his. I licked his bleeding lip, and he moaned. I wanted that sound, I loved that sound that came from him. Stupid boy don't use lip balm. But he tasted so... delicious.

Why couldn't I be immortal?

He was first to break away, gasping for air. Nathan's dark eyes bore into mine, unsure. "What the hell just happened?"

I smiled like a child.

He shook his head, still not able to believe what had just happened. But once he looked into my eyes again, there was a playful smile on his lips too. Nathan leaned forward until his lips were centimeters away from mine. His nose touched my cheek. It tickled. And he pressed his heavenly soft lips to mine.

He had stayed the night, but not that way. We fell asleep on the couch listening to the crackling of the fire. In the morning, I walked him home and he kissed me goodbye. Thank god the day of the storm was Friday, or else we would've been late to school.

Today's Monday, and Nathan didn't show up at school. Right now, I'm sitting on the edge of his bed, looking at his red face, which was cleary over heated. I'm scared out of my freaking mind right now, because that is the first phase of the change. And the thing is, I didn't know if his fever was from the storm... or that he was finally changing.

Bloody Secrets...

"What?" Dad screamed at me as I sat helplessly on our sofa. "He's changing?" I cringed at the word.

"I don't know, dad," I whispered. "I think he finally is."

"Why?" he said quietly, almost like he was talking to himself. "Why now?" Dad paced around the living room, once in a while glaring at Nathan's little old glove. His eyes were full of fright and worry.

"I kissed him," I squeaked, and my dad stopped. This time, his eyes were full of anger. "And... his lip... it was bleeding," I elaborated, and my father's chest began to rise up and down. "I... I didn't know."

Dad looked at me. He had said nothing for several minutes, and I didn't know whether I liked it or that I would prefer him yelling at me, anything. What happens now? We didn't know if Nathan was changing or not, and it was driving me crazy. He might become one of us. I didn't know if I would be happy or scared if that were to happen.

"Does he know?" Dad asked after he sat down on the sofa next to me, his hands rubbing his nervous face. "Does Nathan know?" he said again.

Tears were so close to falling down. "No," I croaked. "He doesn't."

"Go tell him," he said, nearly crying himself.

I shoot my head towards him. "What? Why?"

"He needs to know what he is, Scarlet. Even if he's not changing, there's a part of him that wants to be, that needs to be. If he doesn't know, his father might be in danger... or he might be in danger." And with those words, my father got up and went to his bedroom.

I drove over to Nathan's house. I bet I could even walk to his house if I was blind; I've been there so many times. But this time, I think this might be my last time here. He might never want to see me again.

Nathan's father let me in easily. He approves of me, I think. I slowly went up to Nathan's bedroom, my mind already regretting every squeak I make from the stairs. Soon enough, I was at the door. My heart wanted to jump out of my chest, and my head was starting to throb. Before it was too late, I turn the door knob and looked at Nathan's red face.

He winced at the sound of the door; it needed some oil. But when he saw that it was me, he forced a warm smile. "Hi," he whispered.

"Hi," I said, my voice cracking. Walking into his room, all I smelled when his smelly Axe. I grabbed the nearest chair, with was a wooden one, and sat next to him. I held onto one of his hands, and my other hand was wiping traitor tears that were already falling.

"Why are you crying?" he asked, worried but smiling. "It's only a fever, Scarlet. You don't have to worry. I'll be back soon enough."

"No," I cried. "No, you won't."

Nathan frowned, wincing as he did it. "What do you mean? What do you mean I won't?"

I kissed his hand and he gave me a reassuring squeeze. My tears fell on his hand, which began to hold my cheek, his thumb wiping the wetness against it. "You won't be back," I said. "Not in the same way. Remember when you ask me what I was?" Nathan nodded. "I'm a werewolf, Nathan."

His eyes didn't widen, and he kept his face clear of emotions. He wasn't surprised or anything. After a moment, he said, "I know."

"What?" I said, whipping my head away from his hand. "How?"

"You know," he said. "The incident in the woods... the arm wrestle ... and your skin burns the life out of me sometimes," Nathan laughs lightly. "I just wanted to be sure I was right. I wanted you to tell me."

I took another breath. "There's more, Nathan. You're a werewolf."

Now his eyes widen, and he begins to sit up on the bed. Nathan gripped my hand tightly as he painfully sat up. "How? How do you know?" he asks.

"When we lived back in Canada, there was a wild fire. My father and I escaped, but that was because I followed him. The rest of the family; my mom, brother, everyone--they weren't fast enough. They died." Tears began to caress my cheeks again. "After that, my dad and I had to start over. He was crazy. And then one day he ran back to our home--the woods. It had snowed, and I followed him. You looked so lost, Nathan, alone. Something snapped inside my father's head, and he wanted to start over another family... starting with you. But he couldn't do it. You were just an innocent child."

Slowly, Nathan's hot shaking hand removed itself from mine. All I felt was a sharp pain in my heart.

"You're the little red wolf," he said, though it wasn't a question at all. He was talking to himself, still not believing. Nathan looked at me frantically, his eyes frightened. No... no... this wasn't how it was supposed to go.

"There's a wolf inside of you, Nathan. But you won't let it out--didn't let it out," I added, and he cringed.

"Why didn't you tell me this?!" he roared, scaring me. His face reddened even more, sweat climbing down his forehead. "There's a creature inside of me! And you knew, didn't you? You knew I was that boy--that boy that your dad nearly killed--you knew!" I looked into his eyes, and what I saw was anger... and revenge. "I had to go through years of therapy, did you know that? My life was black and white. I couldn't stand the presence of a dog until I was nine. And it was all because of you and your father."

"I didn't know, Nathan. I didn't know what my father was thinking. Please," I begged.

"Does it hurt? Does the change hurt?" he asks out of the blue, interrupting me.

I frowned. "At first, yes," I answered in a whisper.

"Great, that was all I needed," he growled to himself.

My hand reached out for his again, but when my skin brushed his, he cringed away from me. He no longer looked angry, scared, or anything. His forest green eyes were dark, but... sad. And then he said two words that broke my heart.

"Get out," Nathan said, wiping a tear from his eyes as he said it. "Please."

The hand that had wanted his dropped. "What? No, Nathan, please. Don't push me away. I care for you. I can help you through this, if you're changing that is. Just don't push me away."

"I don't want you here, Scarlet. You're the daughter of a man--no, a werewolf--that nearly took my life away. I can't do this." And then he said another two words, and the shattered pieces of my heart broke again. "I'm sorry."

You can easily say... I kissed him with all my life.

His lips were boiling, even against mine. It took him seconds for his lips to respond, and you had no idea how much I needed this, how much a wanted this. Nathan's hand caressed my cheeks, which were warm from crying so much.

Soon I broke away, kissing his cheek and forehead. "Don't do this to me, Nathan. Don't push me away."

"I have to, Scarlet," he said, almost instantly. "If you love me, like me, hate me even, please, let me have some peace for a few days. I'm begging you, Scar. Just a few days."

With another kiss on the lips, I found the courage to let him go. I closed the door, and I remember his sad eyes just on the other side of it. I left the house, running to my truck while Mr. Adams asked if Nathan had done anything wrong to me. I nearly laughed at him.

My hand was wet from trying to stop the tears, but I couldn't help myself. Those few days, the few days that he said he needed, I have him those. But you see, they felt like hell. Not only did he break my heart, he took some pieces of it.

What am I?

If there is a wolf inside of me, just dying to get out, why doesn't it already? I wanted to laugh, but I felt to weak to. Listen to me, I'm in the process of turning into something I've been afraid of. Is it possible to be afraid of yourself? Will I ever look at myself the same?

I was becoming a monster.

Now I lay weakly on my bed, which wasn't helping at all. Every time I turn to a different side, it would already be warm. I wanted to cool down, physically and mentally, not to mention emotionally. Why... why did it have to be Scarlet and her father? Of all the werewolves in the world, of all the places my dad wanted to move in, we would clash together, ten years later. This wasn't a fairytale at all; this was a nightmare.

I gave him three days alone.

After those three days, I came to visit, but I couldn't say hello. Though he was over-the-top boiling, he was in his bed, pale as ever. I could barely hear his heartbeat, which was slowly beating by the second.

Stop fighting, Nathan. Stop fighting your wolf self. I tried to speak to him through my thoughts. C'mon, you can't die. Don't die on me.

Being a wolf is cool, even if one tried to turn you. You can fight my dad back if you want, Nathan, just don't die.

Ahh... I heard a faint groan.

Nathan?

On the bed, he cringed, but even doing that, he was weak. I came and kneeled next to the bed, clutching onto his hand, and he squeezed back weakly.

Scarlet, he called. It sounded like a whisper in my head. It hurts.

Don't fight it then. I scold.

I wish I could see you. I can't open my eyes. After a moment, he added. I miss you.

I kissed his hand. I miss you too.

Driven Away

His hand no longer held onto mine; it was limp. I couldn't feel his heartbeat against my palm anymore. I didn't hear it. His chest had stopped rising. Hesitantly, I raise my fingers to the bottom of his nose, and nothing, not even a weak breath, was let out.

Panic. That's what people do, right? But I sure didn't feel like panicking. I couldn't. Nathan can't be dead. Not now.

Is it that bad? Is it that bad to become a creature that nearly killed you--to become the creature that has scarred you for life? Would you rather become your worst nightmare or die? There was a choice. And I guess Nathan chose the second.

I wanted to do something. I really did. But as I said, I couldn't. His face was flushed from the warmth inside of him, the him that wanted to come out so bad. Nathan was finally cooling down, peacefully in his sleep. I never thought I grew to like this boy, much less care for him.

I still don't know why he didn't change. Did the doctors do something to him? Was it the hospital that made the wolf inside of him temporarily run away? Or was it just Nathan, fighting against himself? As these questions run through my mind I realized that Nathan's hand was still in mine, and that I am panicking.

"Nathan," I said, finding my voice. "Nathan," I called again as I hit his cheek softly. "Wake up, Adams." I seriously was going to shake him awake until I heard his faint voice in my head.

Bye, Scarlet.

And Nathan was no longer with me.

I heard her footsteps, echoing louder and louder against my ears. I heard her from the creak of the stairs to the creak of my bedroom door. It was so peaceful, so quiet in the room, that Scarlet's shoes sounded like pure thundering.

It was freaking hell.

I was too weak. The fever had taken over completely. My eyes--I couldn't open them. My body--I couldn't move it. The only thing I was able to do was think, but my head was numb. Everything felt numb actually.

Soon the footsteps came to an end, and I nearly died searching for another sound. I thought death had finally taken over. But soon a warm hand held onto mine (as if I wasn't already hot enough) and it sent tingles up my arm.

Scarlet was quiet, but all I needed was her here. As mad as I was, I can't be mad at her. I've been alone, hiding from what I truly was, even if I didn't want to be it. I don't want to be alone anymore. Do you know what it feels like? To be hiding not only from yourself but from... life in general? And now look at me--I'm more trapped. I'm trapped in my own body.

She squeezed my hand, and then a faint voice in my head began to grow.

Stop fighting, Nathan. Stop fighting your wolf self. It was Scarlet's voice... in my head... This was wickedly creepy... C'mon, you can't die. Don't die on me. Being a wolf is cool, even if one tried to turn you. You can fight my dad back if you want, Nathan, just don't die.

She really did care.

I didn't know how to reply in my head. Do I just think what I would say? Suddenly, I felt a sharp pain in my heart. Literally.

Ahh... I tried to groan, but nothing came out. As I said, I was weak.

Nathan? I heard her again.

Scarlet... it hurts. I whined.

Don't fight it then. She said.

After a moment, the air I was breathing was getting harder to get. I squeezed out as many words as I could in the breath I had left. I wish I could see you. I can't open my eyes. I miss you.

I miss you too. Scarlet said as I felt her lips press against my hand.

And soon there was nothing left to feel, to see, to hear. It was just the darkness taking me in.

There was something familiar in the air. It was the smell of the woods that made my spine shiver inside, that made it want to shrink. I listen carefully to the voice in my head. "Nathan... Nathan... Wake up, Adams." I automatically cringe at the name, though I didn't know why.

And out of my control, my head speaks for me. Bye, Scarlet.

The wonderful darkness took me in again.

"Dammit, Adams! I know you're still in there! Get out!" the voice yelled. "Nathan!"

I was laying on... I don't know, but it was uncomfortable. My hand twitches, trying to feel around me. What I felt within my fingers was like a thin piece of paper, but it was crunchy, and it turned into ashes as I fist it within my weak hand. Where was I?

Failing to sit up, I begin to feel somewhere else. I digged my fingers into something cool, moist even, and I instantly knew where I was. I was in the woods.

Opening my eyes, I find a pair of grey eyes looking into my green. But to my surprise, I wasn't afraid of them anymore. They were just... beautiful.

Scarlet looked at me with hope and fear in those eyes, and I didn't blame her. I was feeling the same way. Do you know how much I'm hoping that I won't die? Do you know how weird it is that I wanted to see those pair of grey eyes again? And do you know what it feels like to be afraid of what you might become?

"Nathan!" she screamed with a nice tearful smile.

"Hey, Scarlet," I croaked softly. It sounded like I haven't spoken in years. "How long..." I wanted to ask, but the air seemed thicker again, even though I was in the woods.

"Only a few hours..." Scarlet answered, her tone full of worry. "Stop fighting it," she cried.

I winced as her words hit my ears. "I don't want to be a werewolf..."

"You don't want to die, do you?" she screamed at me. "For everyone, Nathan, let it happen. It's not going to be that bad. I swear, Nathan, if you die, I'll kill you!"

Even in this state, I laughed. "That doesn't even make sense."

"I'm serious. Keep fighting it, and you'll think it will be the biggest regret of your life. Everything you've been through will be for nothing." I wanted to protest, but Scarlet gave me no chance to. "You said that you felt trap, right? This is a way to fix that. Being a wolf is like an escape. Once you're out here, there's nothing to care about. It's just the feeling of finally being free. Don't you want that, Nathan?"

"I do... but I'm not the one controlling all of this, Scarlet. I think he is. It's not like I want to die. He's just taking his goddamn time! I swear, I'll live... I'll change. I won't die. Believe me. I wouldn't do anything to leave you." I didn't regret that last sentence.

Her expression was so... her. There was shock in those eyes, yet full of love too. Not to be lovey dovey or anything, but my heart fluttered. My freaking dying heart fucking fluttered. It was the second best feeling in the world. But the very first best feeling in the world was what she said to me after.

"I love you, Nathan."

And in that moment, the light that I woke up to, darkened. The full moon above me started to appear, and her grey eyes litted with fear as she noticed the sudden difference in that moment. I wondered so much if mates were real.

Without hesitation, I held her hand and said a sentence I will never break. "I'll start over with you."

The last thing I saw was her teary eyes, her head shaking back and forth, not believing what was happening. Her red hair and grey eyes were the last thing I remember seeing as the darkness once again took me back in. I started to wonder again what was really happening to me, and if this was my destiny or if there was any such thing like it.

I wasn't afraid anymore. I wasn't afraid of those scared eyes or wolves or anything. I felt infinite-- powerful, even if I wasn't the one in control. I had a new dream now, and it was to start over with Scarlet. I'll start a new pack, a new family.

Soon enough, I was driven away... from myself.

Stupid, Unstable Paws

He fainted again, but at least I knew he was alive. I had taken him out into the woods so he could turn, if he was going to anyways. It was easier to change out here. Plus, you wouldn't look like a crazy dog running around in the house. And your father wouldn't run away from you...

Nathan laid on the ground peacefully, cooling down from the cold, fall air around him. It was nearly winter, and winter was always a sad season for me. You know, because of the fire and stuff. But with the things that Nathan had just said a few minutes ago, maybe this year's Christmas wouldn't be so sad.

Maybe I can start over with him, this time with no sadness or guilty feelings deep inside of me. Maybe Nathan will get over his fear of wolves, because he will become one. And maybe, just maybe, he will be my mate. We'll spend the rest of our lives with our crazy history, and it would have started just when we were seven.

Though now that I think about it, this was some sad fairytale.

Just probably a month ago this boy was the most annoying thing in the world, but... he has made such an effort to be my friend, I can't hate him. In fact, I was the first one to say 'I love you'. But I'm very afraid that he doesn't love me back. Simply because... he didn't say it back.

But I don't need his love (yet). All the guilt I had, it just disappeared when he said those wonderful words. "I'll start over with you." Those words give me a chance. I gave him a chance to be my friend, and now he has given me a chance to give back his life--one that is not full of nightmares and scars. You have no idea how thankful I am right now.

This fairytale of ours seem short now that I think about it. There was this gap in our lives--the time we were apart. We were both scarred from the stupid wildfire that took place in Canada. And then--now, we meet again. Is this God's way of telling us we are meant to be?

All of these thoughts rush through my mind, and I don't know whether I'm right or wrong. But soon, if... when Nathan changes, I will know how our fairytale ends.

I was starting to itch everywhere.

But the thing was, I couldn't scratch it. It was like a scratch that was inside of me, and you can't really touch what's inside of you.

Oddly, I was conscious but unconscious. That's the only way I could describe it. I was aware that I was in the woods, and that Scarlet was the warm body I felt next to me, but I couldn't move. I wasn't in control of my body. It was.

And it was getting goddamn annoying.

My hand started to really itch, and I wanted to scratch it so bad. And then there was this burn in my toe, and it shot all the away up to my head. Is this was changing feels like?

Soon I really did feel the change. I was sweating in the freaking cool weather, can you believe it? I could feel my heart speed, and I swear I thought I really was going to die. But no... luckily I didn't. My body began to heat up, and the burn of my body turned itchy and irritating. I couldn't do anything though, the warmth of my body kind of made me stiff. Getting really annoyed, I tried to move.

Boy did that hurt.

The first bone to crack was my fucking shin. And then the other. Being the freaking man I was, I cried out the indescribable pain, hoping I was only crying in my mind (because even Scarlet seemed manlier than me...). Soon I could feel all the bones in my body shatter into tiny little pieces, and then joining together in unusual clumps.

I'm sorry, I really suck at describing things.

The only thing that stayed in place was my heart, which still kept beating faster by the second. Though I was too distracted to really even feel it. Would you like to know why? My face felt like it was being mushed together.

I don't even want to describe the pain in my nose right now...

After feeling my face being mushed together, I couldn't feel anything else. I was still breathing, thank god. (No seriously, I thought the devil was torturing me in complete darkness.) I struggle to open my eyes, and I succeeded.

The darkness didn't blind me, so I guess it was good that I changed in the night. At least, I think I changed. I found that my cheek was faced to the dirt... that's what it felt like. Everything seemed pretty blurry. But when everything became clearer, I freaked out.

I crossed my eyes, and I saw my nose... a wolf's nose. It was furry... and wet. Ew... it felt sort of weird. Suddenly I was able to smell... well... everything. Everything became sharper, clearer, and even brighter in the night.

I changed... I had really changed.

Indeed, I was laying on my side, and it felt really awkward. As I try to stand up, I find that I definitely cannot keep balance. It was like I had to left feet!

Oh... wait... I do.

Huh.

Anyways, I kind of wobble on my stupid, unstable paws. And... I'm telling you this now, I bumped into a tree trying to balance myself. That was when I heard a small giggle near.

Scarlet was right in front of me, leaning against a tree. I, on the other hand, was plopped down back on the ground, dazed. Next to her were my clothes, folded neatly next to her shoes. And then another thought hit me... Did she unclothe me?

Yes, I did. Her voice said in my mind. Nothing interesting though, since you've already seen me naked.

My eyes widened, and I see a smirk on her pretty lips. You're enjoying this, aren't you? I asked her.

A little bit, yes. At first I felt a little sorry for you, but this is just too funny. Scarlet said, and laughed out loud. Try to get on all fours, and move around without picking up your paws. When you think you can balance, try walking.

I did as she said, and it helped... a lot. It was a lot better than crashing your body into a tree. Soon enough, I was jumping around, and even tried to stand on my two back legs. I succeed like a pro.

For once, I actually felt free.

I heard a noise, like a branch breaking, and I noticed that Scarlet was no longer in my sight. I searched for the noise maker, but I didn't really need to. From the tree she stood in front of, a red wolf emerged from behind. Her grey eyes glittered and sadly, I didn't know if I could smile as a wolf, but I tried anyways.

Scarlet walked to me, and then tilted her head to a side.

Out of nowhere, she licks my nose.

It seemed really disgusting at first, but it was soothing feeling when I did it back. Soon we were kissing (wolf kissing), licking each other to be exact. I had to admit, it was kind of better than French kissing. After we broke apart, her eyes squinted, indicating she was smiling.

And then she said something that gave me an adrenaline rush.

Let's have a run, shall we?

It was the best run of my life.

When Nathan changed back, the first thing he said was "I feel like jelly." Yeah, if you wanted to know what changing back feels like, it feels like you're being stretched. A whole lot.

There were golden rings around the pupils of his eyes, and that would only last a while. It only takes a few changes for those to go away. But still, those eyes looked beautiful on him.

And I couldn't help but love him more for doing this for me.

We changed back, but it was kind of awkward since we saw each other... uh... naked. Scarlet quickly grabbed her clothes and went behind a tree to change, while I kind of just stood there, feeling like jelly. I guess she was shy to change in front of me.

And sadly, I kind of was too.

After we changed into our clothes, the first thing I said was...

"I feel like jelly."

"Well, it'll be better after a walk home," she said, tying her shoes.

"But I'm tired," I whined, and she looked up at me, rolling her eyes.

We did walk home, well, it wasn't really home now. It was just a place to... be who you're not.

Scarlet was giving me a How to Be a Werewolf 101 lecture on the way and I was feeling really, really excited. But soon we reached the house, and Mr. Perez's eyes widened at the sight of me even standing, much less walking.

He opened the glass door, looking at me. I knew that my eyes were golden now, and I desperately wanted to see them. But, business first.

"Mr. Perez," I said in a serious tone.

"Nathan," he whispered, still not believing.

"We need to talk."

Like a Madman

"We need to talk," was what Nathan said.

Those four words made one of the scariest sentences ever made. It was a sentence used for when you are in trouble, when someone breaks up with you, and when a kind person is trying to help you. But those four words were never used in situations like these.

There is a rumor within all of the werewolf stories I've read. And that rumor is that one must kill the alpha to become the alpha. I have to say, that is true. But what if the alpha doesn't want to be an alpha anymore?

Do you know what it feels like to lose your mate? No, my parents weren't soul-bonded. But losing your mate makes you weaker, I know that--I've felt it. It feels like there's a voice missing in your head, and you would find yourself talking to... well, yourself. You feel empty, and hollow inside, because a part of you is just... gone.

Ever since my family has died my father made no attempt to create another one, with the exception of Nathan of course. He couldn't fill in the hole inside his heart. In the same day as the fire, he was no longer an alpha. I was a survivor in that fire, and I could see it in his eyes, that he could no longer do it. Mom wasn't there to speak with him, to comfort him, to support him. It was pointless.

I never really had a family again, and that's probably why I'm bubbling with excitement.

Now we're sitting in the living room, Nathan staring intently at my dad, and as I look at him, he seemed to be crumbling on the inside.

"I'd like to say something to you, Mr. Perez," Nathan said. "Thank you."

My dad blinked, surprised. "Pardon?"

"Thank you, sir. I'm finally free. I'm finally who I'm meant to be."

"But all the pain I've caused you..." My father whispered, still confused. Suddenly he looks up onto the wall where Nathan's little old glove was hung, and I knew memories were attacking him again.

"All the pain... compared to this feeling... there is no comparison." I was touched by Nathan's words, even if it had nothing to do with me. "But, I have one thing to ask you."

Without any hesitation, my father replied, "Anything, Nathan."

"Would you... would you please by my beta?" he asked, unsure of his terms.

My father's eyebrows furrowed. "Beta..." he whispered, but I'm sure he knows the term by heart. "You mean... you'll become an alpha?"

"I'm starting over my life... with your daughter of course," Nathan said, putting his arm around my shoulders and I couldn't help but shiver. His touch over so warm.

Dad's eyes widened. "No, you can't. You can't start a pack. It's too early for you; you're too young. And... you two have known each other for a month! It's unacceptable! You've changed once, Nathan. Once isn't enough to fight others. It isn't enough to start a family. You're seventeen."

"I'm aware of my age!" Nathan yelled, making my dad and I jump in our seats. "Do you know why I want to start a family? I want to start a family because of your daughter! She doesn't have a family, a home. I know it wasn't your fault the fire happened, but get over it! You're her parent! Parents are there to comfort their children--teach their children. But you, you just keep reminding yourself about that day. She feels it too. She's been reminded too much. I can feel her pain. What's the point of that?" He rushed all of those statements together so quickly I thought I couldn't follow, but I didn't need to. I felt his anger, and my heart swelled.

"Don't you think I know that?" my dad said with his cracked voice. "Don't you think I want my family back?"

"Then do something about it!"

"I can't!" My dad started to yell now. "My soul is broken, you bloody idiot! My wife is dead! My family is gone! Nothing will ever compare to them! Nothing!"

The room became quiet; no one had anything to say. I haven't said a thing since I set foot in the house, not even a hello to my father. I feel undoubtedly useless right now in the conversation.

"I'm sorry, sir," Nathan apologized, but then said one of the most painful sentences. "But it's time to move on." With those simple words he got up and left the house, leaving my father and I in awkward yet sad silence.

As I walk out the door, the cold wind hit my face, but I wasn't affected by it. I was too warm now. The night was calm, unlike me right now, just boiling on the inside. I know I was pretty cruel in there... but I couldn't control myself. I've been having that problem lately, and it's driving me pretty insane.

All I wanted to do was start over and no longer live in fear. I didn't want to live in my old world, simply because my old world was full of nightmares. When a grey-eyed person look at me, I would shrink in fear because I would be remembered of the wolf attack. But I'm not afraid now. I can't be, because I want to spend the rest of my life with Scarlet. I want to give her everything I've got.

What am I supposed to do now? How was I going to start a family?

You know... The perverted voice inside my head said.

You idiot, I mean a pack. I have to bite people and shit, I'm not going to do the dirty with Scarlet. Yet... I try to swallow down my last word, though it was really hard not to smile. I gotta admit, she was a bitch when I met her (no pun intended), but in just a month, we're here now. We're not enemies, we're...

What are we?

This much thinking, in my opinion, was not healthy at all. I don't know what question to answer first. And as if my mind wasn't full enough, another question popped into my head.

How am I going to tell dad? Mom? Should I tell them at all? They would probably be like: "Stop reading those werewolf stories, Nathan. Do something and be a man for once." Euk, I don't like the sound of them in my head. Annoying I'm telling ya.

Soon I reached home--well, not really home anymore in my eyes, but I got nothing else to call it. The door seemed to haunt me now, since my dad was right behind it. How was I going to explain this to him? I bet he's just going to be amazed that I'm alive after having a fever for a whole week. I'm surprised I'm alive too.

I was going to open the door, but my father opened the door for me. "Nathan," my father whispered. Jeez, is everyone going to react like that? Are they really that surprised that I'm alive?

"Dad," I greeted. "What's up?" I really want to slap myself right now.

"What did she do?" My dad said, touching my hair, examining my face. "You were practically limp in Scarlet's arms last time I saw you, boy, what did she do? You're practically healthy now!" Scarlet carried me? What the fu--

"You've got one hell of a girlfriend, Nathan," dad said, still touching my face to see if I'm really alive. But I smiled at his words... girlfriend.

Hell yeah, I'm the best girlfriend you got, idiot. Better believe it now. Her voice popped into my mind.

The telepathy thing is creepy as fuck. You can hear anything in my mind, right? I feel so exposed. I joked.

It's best that I know what you're thinking. Who knows? You might become an ass and cheat on me. This is the safest way to have a relationship with you. Nobody knows what you're going to do... well... except me, of course. She said, and I felt her smiling to herself.

Oh, the things I'd do to you. I joked.

Nathan! She yelled, and her voice practically echoed in my head. I chuckled at her reaction.

"Nathan, why are you laughing to yourself? Did Scarlet drug you or something? Is that why you're like this? Please tell me you're not hanging out with drug buddies," my dad interrupted our conversation.

Drug you? What the fuck? What happened to one hell of a girlfriend? I saw her pouting with that voice in my mind, and I couldn't help but chuckle again.

"It's nothing, dad. She didn't drug me and I don't have drug buddies. My thoughts are just going crazy right now." It wasn't a total lie.

"You should probably get some rest," dad said after eyeing me. "You missed school and you need to catch up tomorrow."

Oh yeah, school. Wait, what? Aw, man, not school! Dammit.

"Okay," I said, keeping all of my whiny thoughts to myself. "Night."

"Night, Nathan," he said, and then went into his little home office, probably finishing up some paperwork.

I went up to my room and got ready for bed, like he said. But I couldn't sleep. Scarlet was talking to me, and we were having a conversation on practically everything. I guess I didn't really mind having her in my head, it was... kind of sweet... My heart warmed at the thought. I wouldn't mind this at all. I wouldn't mind having her by my side for the rest of my life. She's just like the wolf part of me... she was the part that was missing for so long.

And soon, I went to sleep, having no more fears but with the sound of Scarlet's voice, singing like an angel.

School was no longer scary, well, not as scary as yesterday. I felt finally relieved. Nathan was no longer sick. And that is the best feeling ever. To be carefree, that is the best thing ever.

I was getting ready for first and second period, unloading all the unneccessary shit out of my backpack. That is, until I felt a warm pair of hands on my waist. I knew instantly who it was, simply because he didn't cut down the Axe like I told him too.

"Mornin'," he said, his deep voice making the butterflies in my stomach flutter.

"Mornin'," I copied him. He kisses me on the cheek and finally lets go, but it felt like his hands were... oddly... meant to be there, meant to be on my waist.

Soon I was done with preparing for class, but I didn't bother waiting for Nathan. I simply said, "See ya in class."

And his reply was, "See ya." I swear I saw him smirk.

Classes went by smoothly and soon enough it was lunch time. I could already tell I made a good decision on bringing my lunch today, because the lunch ladies were making their meatloaf. And trust me, you don't want to try their meatloaf.

I got my lunch out of my locker and shut it. Though when I turned around I was face to face with Nathan, who was looking so calm it was kind of scary.

"You should share your lunch with me," he said, his nose wrinkling. "That smell is horrible."

"Welcome to my world," I said, smiling. Before I knew what was happening I was pressed up against my own locker, frozen. "Nathan..." I warned. I felt all the eyes in the hallway on us, but it didn't seem like Nathan cared.

"I love your world," he said, and he kissed me. It was a soft kiss, a slow... seductive one. I was kind of dying on the inside of how natural this felt. But then, he stopped.

There was a pain inside my head, and it was starting to grow. I thought it was a headache at first, but boy I was wrong. It was a pain I had experienced yesterday, the pain of changing.

The pain was starting to threaten me, and I broke the kiss. Scarlet's eyes grew worried, and I was too. "Scarlet," I whispered so only she could hear. "I need to change... now." I was panting, and each second the wolf inside of me would give me another shot of pain.

Her grey eyes widened, and she nodded, understanding. "Run," she whispered. "They can't see you turn, run, Nathan."

I could no longer stand the pain inside of me and I indeed ran down the halls, shoving the bodies I see away. And when I was outside of the school, I ran into the darkness place I found, finally letting myself go.

Thank god it wasn't as painful as the first time.

Nathan has been missing for two days. Everywhere I look, every channel I flip to would have Nathan running out of the school.

"This is the second day Nathan Adams has been missing. He was last seen in Jackson High, running out like a madman. No one else saw where he went, and the police are still searching for him now. If you have any information on Nathan Adams, please call now," the news guy said.

Nathan, where are you? I tried asking for the hundredth time, but there was no reply. Please, Nathan...

Home. A voice answered, but he disappeared quickly. He wasn't home though, his dad had told me. Home. Where was... oh, home.

Now I'm standing in front of Nathan's dad. His eyes were full of worry, yet there was anger too. "What are you doing here, Scarlet? Do you know where my son is?" he asked.

And with a intake of air, I answer. "Yes, I do."

Since Seven

It seems that I don't know who I am anymore.

There are two sides of me, the wolf and the human. One doesn't listen to the other, but yet they both want the same thing. I can't control myself, though I didn't really have much of a controlled life in the first place. It's like a tug of war between human-me and wolf-me, and it's annoying.

I need a different word for annoying...

The human-me likes the wolf-me, well, more of what the wolf-me does. But it seems like the wolf can never be in control. I guess it's because the wolf in me has been trapped inside for so long.

I never planned for my life to be like this, for it to be confusing and difficult. Just a few days ago I was complaining about how hard homework was. But never did I think how hard this would be. I'm pulling myself apart, and it's... painful. It's not physically painful, but... emotionally. I want to live a normal teenager life, yet... I want to go out and run, and live. I want to run out into the forest--the woods, and know that I can go on forever, that my home would go on forever.

And that I would be safe.

To be honest, I've always been afraid. Ever since the incident in Canada, there was something inside of me that said "Don't trust them, they can hurt you." And I believed the voice in my head. Right now, I'm wondering if that voice is the wolf inside of me.

I used to love animals. In the woods in Canada, I used to have a dog. Did you know that? But she had to go away because of me. Her name was Locki.

It was just a normal snowy day, and I saw this gigantic dog. Sadly, it wasn't a dog--but I was seven. I didn't know what pain really was until it attacked me. I would always cry about not having something I wanted, but I would never cry because of pain. My dad always told me to be a man and not cry. But the stinging pain in my arm was just enough for me to do so.

And ironically, my dad did too. But his tears wasn't just for me, it was for my mother.

I don't trust people easily. And the reason why is very simple. The person you trust can leave and break your heart.

My father took me to the hospital, and I could hear him yell at the doctors when I woke up. He came storming in the room, slamming the door. The sound was painful in my ears, but it wasn't as painful as when I saw my dad cry. He looked startled to see me awake, and I saw two things in his eyes: hope and sadness.

Dad came over to the scary white bed I was laying on, and hugged me. Giving me a back rub, he silently sobbed, but I didn't say anything.

"I'm fine, Dad," I croaked, but he only shook his head.

Pulling me away, Dad kept a firm grip on my shoulders. With his eyes red, he told me, "I'm sorry, Nathan. Your mother's gone up to sing with the angels."

My eyebrows furrowed. "Why?"

Despite the tears going down his face, he laughed. Though it wasn't a happy laugh; it was more of a fuck-my-life kind of laugh. "She ran a red light. So remember, Nathan, don't speed." Then Dad went to the bathroom and stayed in there for about twenty minutes.

All I did in those minutes was thought about his words. I knew that she was gone, I knew what my Dad meant. But the thing I didn't know what why. Why did my mom have to go? Why her? Of all people, why her?

She died because she sped a red light, to get to me. I killed my own mom.

I remember going to see her for the very last time. I held her cold hands, but I wanted more. I wanted to see her green eyes again, I wanted to see her warm smile. I wanted to be in her comfortable arms. I needed her, but she just wasn't there.

Remembering when I asked myself how I was going to tell mom? Well, I am now.

With the snow beneath my paws, I look at my mom's beautiful face on her headstone. A tear strolls down my furry face, and I hear her voice inside my head.

Nathan... I didn't know... Scarlet said. I'm sorry.

A sigh escaped my nostrils and cold cloud appears from me. And slowly, I fall asleep next to my mother. I really do think she's singing with the angels.

I was going on a road trip.

I brought some food, clothes, and I will be staying over at my Grandma's (on my mother's side) house in Canada. I didn't think I would want to kill any innocent creatures if I ran to Canada, though I can. I'm surprised Nathan's even alive. I'm on the endless highway now, and I was going in at a rest area.

When I got out, my mind was on plenty of things. One of them was why Nathan ran away, especially all the way to Canada. Another thing was why the idiot didn't drive there if he wanted to go so badly. He didn't even take a few bucks with him for food!

As I was driving in my good ol' truck, I begin to see faint images in my head. And what I saw wasn't the most beautiful thing. It went from blood, to tears, to headstones. Nathan's mother's headstone. It was really hard to drive with tears in your eyes, but I managed. He didn't tell me any of this. I didn't know. I knew it was odd that I didn't really see her when I went to Nathan's house, but I always assumed she was at work.

I didn't know what to say.

And I look at the endless road before me, the night beginning to show itself as the sun settle down into a beautiful sunset. Even though I didn't know her, with Nathan's pain inside of me, I too believe she is singing with the angels right now.

I came upon a snow-covered cemetery. All I saw was the snow and the peeking headstones, giving me little chills up my spine. I parked my truck and came out, breathing in fresh air for the first time in the last twenty-four hours. I know Nathan was still here, I could smell him. Knowing that it was going to be a difficult journey, I pass through the cemetery, searching for a specific headstone.

You know, ever since Nathan changed, I've wondered why he wasn't his color. Usually, if you're a werewolf, your fur would be the same color as your hair. But Nathan, his fur was pure white. It was as white as the snow beneath. Thus, it was difficult to find him.

But indeed, I found him.

Nathan was in his wolf form (I really doubt he would want to be a naked human in this freezing weather). His head was tilted to the side, and I know he heard my footsteps. Walking forward, I sit in the snow next to him, looking at his mother's headstone.

The first thing he said to me was, Do you know why we're mates, Scarlet?

I was surprised. Of all things he could've said, he asks me a question that made me speechless. Why? I ask, curious.

Your father may have bitten me, but you cleaned my blood. There's a part of me inside of you. He was quiet until, All I'm missing is a part of you.

I'd be lying if I said I wasn't nervous. I was freaking out. Playing with my fingers, I croak, "We're soulbonded, Nathan. Well, partially."

Even as a wolf, I could see his smile in those forest-green eyes. We were soulbonded since seven. The thought made me smile too. *To be honest, Scarlet, I don't care.* I began to frown, but then I saw a hint of playfulness in his eyes. *I don't care if you can feel what I feel, hear what I hear, I just need you. I just need you to do the same. I want to know what you feel, what you think about. Nothing else matters.*

I couldn't help it, I had to ruin his little romantic confession. "Since when did you get so mushy?"

Nathan turned his head to me and rolled his eyes. *Really, Scarlet? Really? I'm pouring my heart out and all you can do and make fun of it. That's real nice. Note the sarcasm.*

"You know I love you," I said aloud, putting my arm around him.

He turned to me. *Do you really?*

Smiling, I answer. "I do."

And then, Nathan licked me cheek. "Ew! Nathan!" I screamed, laughing.

I love you too. He said, and it sounded like heaven in my head. *You love my kisses. Don't deny it.*

I'm not denying, I'm complaining. You got slobber all over my face. I mean, I know I'm sexy and all but you didn't have to drool. I grin to myself, proud.

He was quiet again. *Hmm... you are sexy.* I didn't care, I shoved him. Hey! That was a compliment!

"Yeah, well, you sound like a pervert," I said and Nathan just rolled his eyes again. "So... how did you survive your long journey here?"

He groaned. I think I need to change my diet. I can never look at a rabbit in the eyes ever again.

"Going vegetarian already?" I joked.

Yep.

I didn't say anything else; I just petted him and scratch his ear. He looked like he was drowning in heaven. No wonder why dogs love this so much, Nathan said and I laugh.

"C'mon, we have to go," I said, getting up.

Where?

"To my Grandma's house. You won't believe this, but it's already winter break. This is just my little short vacation."

Aw, nice! No school!

I began walking back to my truck and Nathan was following right behind. "Yeah, but you need to go change," I ordered, giving him his clothes. "I saw a bathroom around here, but you got the nose, go look for it."

A few minutes later, Nathan came back fully clothed with a pale smile. He was shivering. Oops, I forgot to give him his coat... Not caring, he hugged me and--I'm not going to deny it, I missed his scent--I sniffed him. Nathan gives me a quick kiss and jumps into the truck where the heater was his best friend.

And we were off.

Sleepover Part 1

My grandparents' house never really changed over the years. It was still an old cabin-like house. As I park the car, I see the corner of Nathan's mouth lift, and that made me smile too. It really was a cool house.

Nathan was out of the car quickly, but he stood waiting for me. I got our bags (we were only staying for a few days, I didn't bring much), and started walking to the door with him. When he put his arm around me, I just wanted to snuggle into him. Don't even get me started when he kissed my forehead.

He rang the doorbell, and it didn't take long for my grandma to appear. She had wavy, grey hair, but the eyes of child. They were grey, like mine, but they seemed more innocent, and... younger looking. I don't know any other way to explain them. Her smile was infectious, if you must know, so it was really hard not to smile with her. Nathan didn't even know her, and he was smiling from ear to ear.

"Scarlet, it's been ages," she greeted as she pulls me into her Grandma hug.

When we were broken up, she turns to Nathan, the smile still on her face. "Are you Nathan?" she asks as he nods enthusiastically. I didn't know whether to laugh at his excitement or at his surprised face when Grandma hugged him too. "Wonderful. You should go in the living room and warm up; you guys must be freezing. Come on now," Grandma rushed, and neither of us disagreed with her.

As soon as we stepped inside the living room, I could smell the familiar smell of gingerbread cookies. Did I mention that my grandma is the best grandma ever? Well, she is!

The house was the same on the inside too. There was the old mushy brown sofa, the glass coffee table, outdated TV, and of course the fireplace. Family pictures were hung on the walls. Yep, it was just how I remembered it from last year.

"You two settle in for a little bit, I need to check on the cookies," Grandma said as she walked away.

After she was out of sight, Nathan said, "Those cookies smell good."

"Good won't be the word you'll be using after you eat them," I practically sang.

"We'll see," Nathan said. After a moment filled with the sound of crackling fire from the fireplace, he asks, "Does your grandma know that you're... a... you know..."

"Yeah, she knows. My mom told her everything, Grandpa too." I sigh and took my hair out from my ponytail.

"Where is he?" Nathan asks, looking around. "He's... alive, right?"

I gave him a sad smile. "Yeah, he's alive. But he has this memory problem. One minute he'll remember you, the next he's back into the past. Sometimes he says these random things. It's like his memory doesn't match up to the time period, I guess."

"When did this happen?"

"It was... it was right before the... the fire," I answer nervously, staring at the fireplace. "He was actually pretty cool with it, finding out my mom was a werewolf. Grandma took a longer time to get used to it. But they both accepted my dad and his werewolf family in the end."

We sat down on the little sofa, Nathan's arms around my shoulders. "Forgive me for asking this, but did they..." Nathan began to lick his lips nervously. "Do they blame your dad for your mom's death?"

I didn't know I was so tired until he asked that questioned. I was practically nuzzling into his jacket which smelled heavenly, like him. I guess staying up for a whole day really got to me. "Hmm..." I hummed as I nuzzled closer. "Surprisingly, no. Nobody can really control a wild fire. They were just thankful that... well... I survived," I mumbled.

After a moment, he said, "You must be very tired."

"Here you go kids," Grandma said happily, putting down a plate of freshly baked gingerbread cookies.

"Thank you," Nathan sang, making me chuckle. He took a bite and moaned, and I really began to laugh. "This is delicious!" he exclaimed. "Scarlet, eat one."

MAYBE

I shook my head and stood up from the sofa. "Actually, Grandma, I think I need to rest for a while. You guys can have dinner without me. Sleep's the first thing I need right now. Is that alright with you?" I ask.

Grandma smiled. "Of course, dear. You know where the guest room is. Go on ahead."

I grab our bags and went upstairs to the guest room, walking in with a long, tired sigh. The king-size bed felt like a cold cloud when I flopped onto it. Other than that, I slipped into sleep. The last thing I heard was Grandma laughing at something Nathan had said.

I woke up to the smell of something disgusting.

That was odd. Usually Grandma's house had the smell of pine trees or lemon. But this smell was really... not good.

"Aw, eeewwww," a voice groaned.

Soon I noticed the light coming from the bathroom. The door was slightly opened, so I opened it even wider to see what was going on. And guess what I saw?

What I saw was Nathan on the tiled floor, leaning against the nearest wall with sweat on his forehead. In the toilet was... Okay, I'm just going to say that he vomited. And it was not a pretty color. Yeah, let's go with that.

He looks up to me with another groan. "Did I wake you?"

"Are you okay?" I ask, crouching down to him. "What happened?"

"I think the rabbit finally got to me," he croaked. "I'm sorry," Nathan apologized.

I couldn't help but narrow my eyes. "Why are you apologizing? This happens to everyone."

He shakes his head, causing the sweat on his head to run down his face even quicker. "No, it's not that. I just... I just really doubt you'll kiss me after this."

Now, you gotta admit, when a guy is throwing up his guts and on the edge of death, you would think he would be on the floor crying right now. But no, Nathan is the kind of guy that apologizes and doubts nobody will ever kiss him again. How could I not laugh at that?

After I was done wiping my tears of laughter, Nathan gave me a look of panic and began throwing up again. I rubbed his back, trying to sooth him, and I think it helped. "Poor baby..." I whisper. When I looked in the bowl of digusting rare rabbit soup, I flushed the toilet. I was pretty sure he was done for the night. "Stay right here, alright?" I said, and he nodded.

"I don't think I'm going anywhere for a few minutes," he replied.

I walk out of the bathroom and into the bedroom, searching for something in particular. It was dark, so it took me quite some time to look in our bags. I came back in the bathroom holding the bottle that would solve at least a part of his worries. "Here," I said, handing him my small bottle of Listerine Mouthwash.

Even in his weakened state, he rolled his eyes. "Thanks."

I just smiled back and walked out of the bathroom, leaving him so he could do what he needed to do. When he came back, there was this weird combination of scents in the air. It was the smell between mint and vomit. I didn't know how to respond to it.

I was yet to solve another problem. Getting up from the bed, I walk back into the bathroom, grabbing a wash cloth from one of the drawers below the sink. I wet the cloth and twisted it so it was damp. Walking back into the bedroom, I see Nathan on the bed, breathing heavily.

"C'mon, Nathan," I called as I walked towards him. "Take your shirt off."

He turned to me, raising an eyebrow. "Eager, are we?"

Now it was my turn to roll my eyes. "No, idiot. I can't quite figure out if the smell in the room bothers me or not. It's the smell of your clothes, you need to wash 'em." I put the cloth down onto the sheets and began tugging on his shirt.

He was too tired to protest, so he sat up, rubbing his drowsy eyes. "Go on, undress me," he challenged.

Sleepover Part 2

His eyes glittered in the dark bedroom, the mischievousness making my heart thump harder than before. Undress him? All I wanted to do was make him change! Nathan looked at me, a small but noticeable smirk played on his lips. How can someone joke when they had just been in the bathroom throwing up their guts under an hour ago?

He knew what I was feeling right now, he could tell. He didn't need to hear my thoughts to see how I felt about what he said. But even if he does know, I'm not budging.

Game on, Adams.

I copied the smirk he had on his lips, and grabbed the hem of his shirt. He was surprised for second, no doubt, but I could tell there were questions rushing through his head.

Is she really going to do this? Is this a test? How should I play this?

I wanted to laugh, I really did. Those questions went around like a merry-go-round in his head, but I think he forgot that I could hear his thoughts. But I am testing him. Not only him but myself. How far will I go with this?

When I finally agreed to myself that it was useless to think about it, I went on with my plan and slowly raised his shirt. There was nothing that I haven't seen. Nathan, being the weak boy he was, surprisingly had a six-pack. I mean, I wasn't really surprised, but I couldn't help but think about how weak he was when we arm wrestled.

I wonder if he's stronger than me now...

Slowly I raised the shirt higher, and higher... I pulled his arms out and in no time he was shirtless. I playfully touched his torso lightly as I got the wet cloth from the sheets, and he was burning under my touch. I wiped his chest and he hisses as the coldness made contact with his skin.

The cloth was warm after a few seconds since Nathan was so warm. Everything was normal really, nothing weird now. In fact, I felt really comfortable doing this. But then, I saw these marks on Nathan's skin, right above the heart. The scars were a bit lighter than his normal skin tone, and they were a little dented, if you get what I mean.

I ran my fingers over the four scars, trying to figure out what it was. Soon it dawned on me that I should know these marks. The scars were claw marks--wolf claw marks.

My heart really stopped.

Scarlet was frowning.

Her eyes were staring intently at an area of my chest, and it made me wonder what she was looking at. Those eyes moved up to mine, and I could tell there was water in her eyes. What was she thinking about now?

Scarlet's tiny hand lets go of the cold cloth she had held and used that hand to touch the mid-left of my chest. I should've known she was looking at the scars.

"What happened?" she asks in a whisper. "Did... did my dad do this, Nathan?"

I shook my head and held her hands in mine. "He jumped on me pretty hard, yes. I couldn't believe he got through my thick coat... but anyways, it's fine, Scarlet. Stop crying. That was a long time ago," I said, wiping away her little trail of tears.

"I know, Nathan. I know it was a long time ago. But I can't help... I can't help but think about the pain at such a young age. At seven, you should be able to live carefree, live like an actual kid. But you, you lived like everything around you was hazardous, poison, evil. You can't trust anyone, because you think they'll leave. You can't be around grey-eyed people because you think they'll hurt you. They remind you of all the things that happened after you were attacked. It isn't fair for you, Nathan..." she cried.

I grabbed her hands and used them to cup my face, making her look at me. "Stop crying," I said with a sad smile. "C'mon.. stop crying. You've cried too many times for me." Scarlet was crying even harder after I said that... Soon I gave her a pout, and that was when the corner of her lips move up. "C'mon, Scarly.. You know you want to smile," I said in a baby voice. "You gotta finish cleaning me up, remember? There's still my pants you have to take off," I joked.

Scarlet chuckled and took one of her hands out of mine to playfully slap me on my chest, but being her, her "playful" slap hurts like hell. "Ass," she said, wiping her last tears.

"Yes, my ass is very good to look at," I replied, grinning. "Wanna look?"

She slapped me again. "Maybe later," Scarlet said, making my heart skip a beat. She looked like she was dead serious too. Well, that is, until she was laughing at my shocked face. "Kidding, idiot. I'm not doing anything with you until it's legal."

"When's your birthday?" I questioned.

"It's in late February, Nathan. It's December now. That's all you have to know." She smiled as if she had won.

But that sad thing is, she won more than she thought she did. "Damn," I curse. "My birthday is in March!" Waving my arms in the air in exasperation, I plop back down onto the pillows. Seriously, three months is a long wait.

Scarlet moves over to the other side of the bed, leaning against the wall. Her finger begins to poke the side of my cheek. Repeatedly. It got annoying after three pokes. "Look on the bright side," she said.

"Oh yeah? And what would the bright side be?" I asked in an annoyed tone.

"I don't have to think of a birthday present for you," Scarlet says seductively. She slides down onto the sheets and kisses me softly on the lips. But the great thing was, she didn't pull away. Her lips move in sync with mine, slow and sickly sweet.

I wrap my arm around her slim waist, leaving no room between us. I could feel her tiny fingers running through my hair, though I had spent nearly ten minutes in the bathroom trying to fix it. Oh well, sex-hair is better than vomit-hair. You can't disagree with that.

After a while, one of her hands move down to my chest, slightly pushing me away but somehow bringing us closer. I felt her smile against my lips, which she had bitten. A groan escapes me as I felt her nails digging the skin between my neck and shoulder. My hands move under her shirt, and I swear I felt her shiver. And then a moan erupts from her as I run my tongue across her bottom lip. I didn't know how much I loved the sound until she did it again. It was probably music to my ears.

Finally breaking the tiring kiss, my lips move to her neck instead. I couldn't help but take a whiff of her hair though, it smells so much like... home. And to be honest, I think she was doing the same to me.

"I love you, Scarlet," I sigh, hugging her closer to me, if it was even possible.

Her lips move to my cheek. "I love you more."

"I doubt that. You hated me when you first met me," I argue.

"It was probably your freaking Axe smell," she replied, making me chuckle.

"You love it."

"Said no one ever."

"You miss it right now, I can tell," I mumble.

"No... I love your smell right now. Your natural smell. It smells like..." Scarlet struggles to find the word.

"Home," I said, completing her thought, and she hums, agreeing.

There was about five minutes of complete, thoughtful silence. But I wasn't thinking of anything, worrying about anything. It was just the comfortable quietness, taking me in. I felt like I can live now, I can live carefree. My mind was blank as ever, which was a first. There was no need to think.

All I needed to know was that Scarlet's heart was beating next to mine, slowly meeting my pace. We were already one, even if I don't have a part of her in me. And it was one of the greatest feelings in the world.

"Hey, Scarlet," I called, hoping she was still awake. Luckily, she was still awake enough to hum. "You know I'd die for you, right?"

"As much as I love to hear that, I would die if you die, Nathan," she replies sleepily.

"Oh." Great response, Nathan. "Well, just know that I'd do anything for you."

Scarlet didn't reply for a while, and I assumed she was asleep. But then she said three words that made me smile.

"Freaking cheesy Romeo..."

I woke up to the sunlight outside shining on my face, making me warm and not to mention blind. Nathan's arm had been a wonderful pillow, but now i was sweating like a big because of all the heat I was getting. I mean, I know I'm hot and all, but this is getting too literal... (haha...)

My eyelids were still too tired to open themselves, so I turned away from the light and faced Nathan. What I didn't notice was his "little buddy" poking my thigh. I nearly froze, and I think Nathan was awake since he noticed I almost did too.

"That isn't my fault," he groaned sleepily, and I swear it sounded really sexy... "I had a really nice dream..." he said, bringing me closer, and I didn't really mind after that.

"Was I in your dream, Nathan?" Grandma asked.

Wait. Grandma?!

Soon I was laughing my butt off because Nathan fell off the bed looking at Grandma, who was looking at us with a mysterious gleam in her eyes.

Delicious

I woke up when Scarlet started to move.

I really woke up when I heard her Grandma.

And I really, really woke up when I hit my head on the nightstand and crashed onto the floor.

What a nice morning, right?

It's nice seeing your granddaughter in bed with a half-naked hormonal teenage boy and cuddling with him... right? Hahaha... Nope.

Scarlet was laughing her ass off when I fell onto the floor. She was nearly in tears! Not to mention her Grandma giving us this look. It wasn't a bad look though. There was this thing in her eyes that said: I know what you two did. or I was once a teenager too. I don't know. Her eyes were always mysterious, I guess. And happy.

Just like a grandmother.

Scarlet's Grandma had gone off into the kitchen, making all of us breakfast. I will finally get to meet her Grandpa. I don't know why I want to meet him to badly. I wanted to meet all of Scarlet's relatives actually. I only had my dad... Maybe that's why...

Right now Scarlet was bandaging this little cut on the side of my head. It was only about an inch long of a cut. Luckily, it wasn't a deep one. She has been giggling the whole time because the cut reminded her of my face when I fell onto the floor. And to think she was beginning to be nice..

"I am nice," she said, dabbing my bloody cut with a little wet cloth. "This is just too funny."

"Hey, when your boyfriend falls onto the floor with a boner, you help him up," I said seriously, and she broke into a fit of giggles. "It's nice to see that my embarrassment amuses you," I muttered.

Scarlet grinned. "It does, it really does."

We stayed in comfortable silence as she put Neosporin on the cut and put a band-aid on it. Well, it was almost silent.

"Why can't I choose the band-aid?" I asked. "I'm the one with the cut!"

"I don't care, you're getting the Hello Kitty band-aid," she says in a mother-like voice.

"Why does your grandma even have Hello Kitty band-aids?" I questioned, my voice getting louder, and not to mention higher.

Scarlet rolled her eyes. "Stop being so whiny."

"Why not the Toy Story band-aid? That's more manly than the Hello Kitty and the Barbie ones!" This was getting really ridiculous.

"Shut up, Nathan. You weren't really manly in the first place," she replied. Meanie... "You are such a child. Really, Nathan? Meanie? That's all ya got?"

I shrugged and crossed my arms. You know, I really was acting like a child. But it didn't matter now. What mattered was that my poor head had to face the evil white kitten that was currently aiding it. I literally have no idea what I just said... Huh.

Scarlet puts the band-aid over the cut with a wide smile, making me wince. Biting her lip, she leans in to kiss me, and for a second I didn't even care about Hello Kitty. Even if the kiss had only lasted seconds, it was just enough to make me turn my mood around. This girl was pure magic.

"I love you," she says, and I smile. "But I love Grandma's homemade breakfast more," she added shortly after, making me pout. "Let's go, slowpoke."

We walked downstairs together hand-in-hand, and I couldn't help but think she'll trip me or something. I don't think that badly of Scarlet, but seriously, you don't laugh when a person hits their head. Especially if that person is your boyfriend.

Okay, scratch that. I would laugh if Scarlet fell off the bed. Damn.

Scarlet showed me the way to the dining room, but I could've found my own way. I could smell the food already! I am really starting to love my werewolf senses; they're really helpful. And so much stronger.

We walk into a room will a long table, a light green tablecloth on top of it. There were four plates already on the table, each filled with bacon, eggs, hashbrowns, sausage, and mini pancakes.

"I'm going to get fat after this," I mutter to Scarlet as we sat down.

"You have to see what she makes for lunch, it's like a big buffet," Scarlet mutters back.

"You've lived in heaven your whole life," I smirk.

"I wish."

"I've lived in heaven my whole life," a voice says, making us jump in our chairs.

There was an old man across from us, smiling. He had a head full of grey hair, and that's what surprised me. He wasn't bald or anything, not like I had imagine. Probably because of how much he ate everyday... The man had a grey beard too, neatly trimmed. He could go for the look of Santa Claus, but he was quite fit for his age. Not fat, yet not skinny like a regular teenage boy.

"Mornin', Grandpa," Scarlet says with a slight blush.

"Good morning, Scarlet," he said kindly. "Would you mind telling me who this is?"

She smiled, but then it faded as she looked at her breakfast plate uncomfortably. "This is... this is... um..." And then the question of all cliche love stories popped into my life.

What are we?

Scarlet's grey eyes bore into mine, and they looked... doubtful. She was unsure about something, and by the looks of it, she was sad too. What did she think we were? What did I think? Her Grandpa was watching was, one of his eyebrows raised. But the answer was quite obvious. There wasn't anything to think about.

Hesitantly, I put my hand out for Scarlet's grandpa. "I'm Scarlet's mate, Nathan." He shook the hand with another smile and then folded his hands together.

"Nathan," he said quietly to himself. "Nathan..." he repeated. "Okay, Nathan, how do you know you're Scarly's mate? Is she just a high school crush to you? A one-time thing? Or do you know that you'll spend the rest of your long life with her, assuming you know what she is, of course," he asks, and my heart started to beat faster because of my nervousness.

"He's like me, Grandpa," Scarlet answered, squeezing my hand. "He's a werewolf. You can see it in his eyes."

Her grandpa narrows his eyes and looked straight at me, thinking thoughtfully. "That's a pair of eyes you got there, boy," he commented after.

"They're just gorgeous, aren't they?" Scarlet's Grandma agreed as she was bringing out the syrup for our pancakes. "They're different from a normal werewolf's eye though. I just can't put my finger on what."

Scarlet smiled down at her plate, and then up to her grandparents. "He's... different."

"Isn't that what every teenager say?" Grandpa questioned, looking at his wife.

"Fine. He's extra, extra special," Scarlet corrected, blushing. "There's just this thing between us, and I just know. This is not just the butterflies, the day dreaming... it's... it's not even love at first sight. There's no tug in my heart, and my heart doesn't skip a beat when I see him." Within every word she says, I find myself waiting for something good, something that makes our love at least a little bit cliche. "My heart is simply beating with his, matching and waiting for the other. We're one, I have no other way to say it."

There was this serious silence in the air, and my smile was growing wider by the second. One. We're one. You break one of us, and the other is broken. It doesn't matter what Scarlet says, I do feel my heart skip a beat when I'm with her. Screw the butterflies! What I'm feeling doesn't even feel like a zoo! It feels like... like the stars of the night is burning in my stomach, twinkling.

Scarlet's grandparents smile. "Now, that was very touching Scarlet..." her grandmother began. "But are two going to eat hand-in-hand too?"

As we both look down to our hands, Scarlet pulls out first, blushing scarlet. Haha... Scarlet...

Idiot, I heard her say in my mind.

Ah, but you still love me. I replied, and she stayed quiet.

We ate breakfast, talking out some things, like when we were going home (even though I was already home), and what we were planning to do for the rest of the week. Everything was freaking delicious. I was full by the time we were done, and I was hoping so much that I'll survive today. I was really hoping I wouldn't throw up again, and just the thought of the rabbit made me sick.

Then again, I didn't mind Scarlet's company last night.

But... I'd rather she keep kissing me.

The day went by quickly of us playing in the snow. My face was red by the time I was back indoors, but the reason wasn't because of the cold weather. I wasn't really surprise of Scarlet's strength; I was surprised by her aiming. And that girl had accurate aiming. She hit my face with a snowball (she made a mean-ass snowball too) at least five times. I swear, that girl wants my pretty face to be ugly.

Oh yeah, lunch. It really was a buffet.

Scarlet's grandmother was a freaking chef. There were like three different kinds of salad, choices of sandwiches, noodles, even freaking rice. I couldn't list them all. I don't think I want to leave this place. Home or not, I was living in heaven.

It was around midnight when both of us were finally in bed, both facing the window. The night of full thousands of stars, lighting up the city. I had my arms around Scarlet, spooning her gently. She just lets out long, thoughtful sighs, and it made me wonder what she was thinking about.

"Scarlet," I called, my voice cracking at her name. She hums in response. "What're you thinking about?" I asked.

She sighs and turns her body around, facing me. Her hands move up to my cheeks, cupping them with her tiny hands. Slowly, she brings her soft, heavenly lips to mine. As we kissed, I wanted her closer to me, but we only had so much space. We were already close. I was literally on top of her!

Soon Scarlet was moved her hands away and started playing with my hair, tugging it harder every time she moaned, and the sound made me bubbly. I've only heard it a few times, and I was already addicted.

I break the kiss and move up to her cheek, to her ear, breathing her in as I kissed her. My lips follow her jaw line all the away down to her neck, making her pull on my t-shirt, and I could hear the threads of it simply pulling apart in her grasp.

Licking her neck, I gently bite the area, and she moaned again. I repeated what I did, and got the same results. This went on for a while, but then my teeth started to hurt. And then, Scarlet hissed.

"Oh, Nathan," she groaned.

Against my lips I felt this sickly wet liquid, and I recognized it. I could smell it. Scarlet's blood was in my mouth, slowly climbing down my throat. Some of it was dripping on the side of my mouth, and my eyes widen in fear.

"Are you okay?" I asked. "Scarlet?"

"Do it again," she says softly, and I hesitantly did what she asked.

I ran my tongue over the cut that my fangs had made, earning her legs to wrap around my back. I sucked the blood away, but it didn't taste like the normal blood. This blood... her blood... It was simply delicious.

When I was done, I pressed the point of my nose to the side of her cheek, whispering a sentence in nearly every werewolf story.

"You're mine now."

Running Back

This morning was a calm morning. There were no grandmas, no scares, not a thing to disrupt the rise of the rays of light coming from the sun. Scarlet was breathing softly in my arms, her breaths matching mine. I felt warm, fuzzy even. If you haven't felt this feeling, you don't know what love is.

I've been thinking about Scarlet and me. It is really hard to believe what a month can do. I even thought about our subtitle if our story was written. Hate at first sight. Fits, doesn't it?

Who would've thought that a boy who has had a bad history with wolves and had a phobia of grey eyes would become a wolf and be mates with a grey-eyed girl? A little ironic if you ask me...

"Nathan, stop thinking so much," Scarlet whined softly into my shirt.

My eyes widened. "How did you keep your thoughts so quiet?"

She opens one of her eyes. "I was in a pack, ya know. Everybody knows everything. I'm used to this."

I smiled and bury my nose into her hair. Her cheek was burning my skin, and I shivered at the touch. Slowly, I move my head to look at the "hickey" I had given her. "Is it sore?" I asked, rubbing my thumb around it.

Scarlet shrugged, and winced as she did so. "A 'lil bit," she answers after.

I kissed her cheek. "Just like you should be," I mumbled cheekily.

"Sweetie, I love you, but if you keep making perverted jokes like that you won't live much longer in my sight," she said, running her fingers under my shirt. "What time is it?" Scarlet asks sleepily.

I turned around to look at the little wooden owl clock on the nightstand next to me, squinting my eyes to get used to the morning light. "Um... I think it's eight o'clock right now."

After about five seconds of silence, Scarlet and I both say, "Way too early." Our eyes widened as we looked at each other, amusement both in our eyes. "Um..." we say in sync again. "Stop it," we say, and with that came our synchronized sighs. "I'm not even thinking this," we say, and we just stopped talking because this was getting to a very different level of creepy.

Soon, after a good amount of silence had passed, I asked her, "What do you want to do today?"

She shrugged in my arms, and I knew she had winced again. I wanted so much to smile at that, but I kept my cool. "I don't really know. Do you wanna do anything in particular?" she asks. A few thoughts came to my mind immediately, and those thoughts earned

MAYBE 123

a slap on the arm from Scarlet. "Do you wanna take a run? To get used to changing?" she suggested in an annoyed tone.

"M'kay," I replied. "I wouldn't mind that."

"Just let me sleep some more. I feel really tired," she mumbled, and within just a minute she was sleeping in my arms again.

Not for long though, because I got up and began walking around, searching for pen and paper. I succeeded my quest, and went into the living room to think. I'm going to need to keep tracks of the dates and stuff between Scarlet and me. I don't care how girly I sound.

To be honest, I've never really had a girlfriend. Why would I if they can break my heart? So, since Scarlet and I are together, I don't want anything to break us apart. Mate or not, she was still important to me, and every girl needs to feel special.

Hell, I'm a guy and I feel extra-special.

Somehow, after minutes of thinking about anniversaries, a few questions exploded in my head, as usual.

Am I going to marry Scarlet? Why not?

Is it really necessary though? All girls want their dream wedding!

But this is Scarlet... Exactly! It's Scarlet!

I'm still going to college, right? What are you going to do with your life, dumbass?

Be a werewolf? You need money for a wedding, idiot.

Yeah, well... shut up. This is quite sad, not being able to control your own mind.

You know, I don't even know who I'm having this conversation with anymore. Funny, I don't either.

That was literally five minutes of me having a conversation with myself. I felt like a psycho afterwards. I mean, everyone has talked to themselves before, but mine felt... different. It was like I was split into two different Nathans. Talking to wolf-Nathan is difficult.

You're telling me...

See what I have to deal with?

Have you ever had one of those days where you're burning up, but yet you feel cold at the same time? I was having one of those days right now, but this was like... worse.

I had covered myself with the blanket on the bed, trying to warm up. I was just burning inside, and it's a surprise I'm not sweating. On the outside, I was just plain frozen to death. Every time I shivered, I didn't know what I was shivering for, the cold or the hot side?

Ever since I drifted back to sleep, I felt... sick, to be honest. I heard Nathan shuffling around, and I heard him as he left the room. I didn't need to know what he was doing, because I was worrying about myself. But even with the peaceful morning, I knew I couldn't let it go. I listened carefully to his mind, and it touched me how much he cared about us.

But those questions got me thinking too.

Where exactly am I going with him?

After thinking endlessly about our possible futures, it hit me that I didn't care. We can go anywhere. I won't care, just as long as I'm with Nathan. Time will take us where it wants us to go. If it's meant to be then it's meant to be.

Soon my head felt empty yet full at the same time, and I stopped thinking. It was full of emptiness, if that makes any sense. It hurts though. What's happening to me?

I heard Nathan's footsteps down the hall, so I closed my eyes once more. The sound of the door knob turning erupted in my ears, and the creakiness of it made me wince. Under his breath, I heard Nathan walk over and said, "Damn, it's nearly ten."

Time really does fly...

The cover I had over me was no longer over me. The coldness of the air touches my back, but soon someone's torso warmed it up. Nathan hugged me, spooned me for only just seconds, but he notices that I'm... well... I don't know if I'm burning to freezing in his mind.

"Scarlet," he whispers fretfully. "Are you alright?" His hot breath tickled my neck.

Finally, I started to sweat. I stopped faking sleep and opened my eyes, but I was quickly blinded by the light. I shook my head painfully in response.

"What happened to you?" he asks, the pain in the croak of his voice. Nathan puts his hand on my forehead, frowning as he does so. His eyes were full of worry, no doubt. "Scarlet..." he called again.

I drifted back into nothingless.

I'm now stuck in the middle of the highway, lost.

Scarlet was sick, obviously. I had turned up the heat in the truck, but I didn't know if she was actually freezing or hot as fuck right now. I'm scared, very scared.

The sad thing is, I should've taken her to the hospital. But I didn't, because she got a call.

Her phone was ringing some Ed Sheeran song, and the caller ID was 'Bestie', so I assumed it was April. It was. But it wasn't a happy call...

"Hello?" I greeted, looking at Scarlet worriedly.

There was silence. "Nathan?" April asked, unsure.

"The one and only," I croaked. "What's up?"

"Is... is Scarlet there?" April questioned, but she sounded as worried as I was.

"She's... um... sick," I replied. "You want to leave a message or something?"

I heard a sigh on the other line of the phone. "Tell her that her dad's in the hospital."

"What? Why?"

"The doctors don't even know," she sighed again, and then hung up.

Basically, to recap, I'm in the middle of the highway, looking at the map, the GPS, and the gas tank to see if Scarlet and I will survive our trip back "home".

Leaving the Pack

I knew they were mean to be, Nathan and Scarlet, ever since the first day they met. Relationships (especially cliche ones) usually start off with a little argument or two. I didn't think it would come to the point where they become mates though.

I was updated on their relationship only a few days ago, and probably after every sentence Scarlet spoke, my jaw dropped slightly lower. Life sure moves fast when you don't know what the fuck was going on. Well, at least now, I have a chance to be in a pack.

Last night, Scarlet's dad drove himself to the hospital because his chest hurt. As he talked to one of the nurses, he just dropped to the floor, a hand over his heart. He's not dead of course, a heart of a werewolf will always be stronger than a normal human being's. I was notified by call that he was in the hospital. My dad and I had visit him, talked to him and discussed what had happen.

You can't really have a heart attack for no reason. There's always a reason. Scarlet's dad never did anything to damage his heart, so what happened? I'm still thinking about it, but I think I have a pretty good idea what happened.

I think.

Is it possible that Scarlet is a better driver than I am? 'Cause I think so.

She has been shivering and sweating during our trip back, a few complaints here and then. We have only about an hour left till we're back at home. Scarlet said to go to her house first, then the hospital, because she needed to get some things ready.

My eyes are kinda dying right now; I'm so close to falling asleep in this dreadful traffic. When did Missouri have so much traffic anyway? I bet you that I would've been home hours ago on paws. Seriously, that's how slow the traffic is. I'm just a freaking state away.

"Nathan..." Scarlet whispers, her eyes still closed. "How much longer?"

I forced a sarcastic smile. "In this traffic? I'm hoping two hours."

"Damn people," she said in an annoyed tone. "Don't know how to follow laws. Now we're stuck in traffic. Stupid, stupid people."

I drum my fingers on the steering wheel. "This is a plus for criminals though... the police can't catch 'em in this kind of traffic."

She opened one of her eyes. "Is this what you think about at a time's crisis? My father's in the hospital and all you can do is think about the benefits of being a criminal?"

I grinned. "You're the mind reader, not me."

Scarlet closes her eyes again and I can tell that she internally rolled her eyes. I smile to myself at the thought.

"You feeling okay, Scar?" I asked, bored. I still care though, she looked pretty sick.

She lets out a quiet breath. "I haven't felt okay in months. Not since you've entered my life," she says, smiling. "I just... I don't feel well. I'm sick, but I'm also not sick. I don't understand it."

"You were perfectly healthy last night," I whispered, more to myself, but of course she heard it. "How can something like this happen just over night? You being sick.. and your father... he's not so well either..."

Silence filled the truck. Well, with the exception of car honks in the background.

"It does seem kinda strange, doesn't it?" I went on, slowly. "You and your dad, sick at the same time? Quite a coincidence, isn't it?"

"What are you thinking, Nathan?" Scarlet asks, giving her full attention.

"I think something broke between you two."

It hurts. Everything hurts.

But most of all, my heart hurts.

When I lost my wife, I thought that was the worst. I thought that was it, that it couldn't be worse than that. There's no other feeling that can compare to the emptiness in a heart, to the loneliness. Though what I'm feeling now, is not only the loneliness, but the betrayal.

Scarlet is the only family I have left. She's it. She's my daughter, my darling. She's the light of my life, the spirit for me to keep going. And most of all, she's a spinning image of my wife. She's everything, and all I have left.

I can't feel it anymore. I can't feel her essence in my mind. She's just gone.

It was like when Evelyn, my wife, died. I felt weaker, emptier. There was no conscience in my mind, my heart had no reason to beat, life was just completely useless.

It feels like Scarlet died.

It took nearly two and a half hours for us to arrive at my house. The traffic was that bad.

I grabbed some of my dad's stuff, and a little snack. Even though I was not in the mood to eat, I knew that I would much prefer my little snack than some hospital meal.

Before I knew it, we were back in the car again.

May I add, Nathan is quite a slow driver.

We arrived at the hospital. It smells like... clean, but in a dirty way. I don't know how to explain it. It's like the hospital was meant to be clean and all germ-free, but it's not because all of these sick and injured people are in it.

I hate the smell.

And with my werewolf sense of smell, it's much worse. Trust me.

"Euk," Nathan whined, agreeing with my thoughts. "How did your dad survive this?"

I shrugged and asked one of the nurses where my dad was. She knew exactly who I was talking about and led me to him, but before

MAYBE

she could finish leading me, I was stopped at the sight of April. The nurse soon left after that.

"Scarlet!" April greeted, making my head hurt. "Are you alright?" she asks seconds later, worry in her tone.

I shook my head. "I'm f-fine," I said shakily. "Where's my dad?"

April looked unconvinced but nodded and lead me the way anyways. We were at a door in minutes, and everything to me was pretty fuzzy from my dizziness.

"Scarlet?" April called again. But instead of answering her, I shook my head and opened the door.

My died laid on the bed, still and calm. He seemed paler, and he just didn't look alive. "Dad?" I said, unsure of myself.

I saw his hands curl into a fist at my voice. Slowly he opened his eyes. "Scarlet," he sighs.

"What happened?" I questioned, my voice cracking.

"I don't know, Scar," he shrugs. "I just felt really weak last night, so I drove myself to the hospital. But when I came, I collapsed."

I quickly walked over to hug him, but after he began to cough. Soon he stopped though, his eyes on something unpleasant. I looked behind me and all I saw was Nathan and Scarlet. What's he looking at?

I turned my head back to look at him, and I saw anger and hurt in his eyes.

"What is that on your neck?" he asks.

For a second I was confused by his questions, but my hand quickly comes up to cover the hickey on my neck.

Oh shit... I heard Nathan curse. Fuck...

"Um..." I didn't know how to answer his question.

"Did Nathan mark you, Scarlet?" Dad questioned.

"Dad, I--"

"What did you do to her?!" he roared at Nathan.

Nathan's eyes widened for a moment. "Look, Mr. Perez, we didn't--"

"Would you like to know what happened to me, Scarlet?" my father asks, hatred in his voice. "I went weak because of you! You left me! You left the pack!"

My eyebrows furrowed. "What pack?"

"You left me," he said.

"You're not a pack, dad. You're not an Alpha," I said slowly, reassuring myself.

He shook his head. "You don't understand! I was the only one left from the pack, aside from you. We were what was left of the pack! But you left me, and went into another pack. With Nathan," my dad explained.

Now it was my turn to shake my head. "Dad... Nathan's not in a pack... we weren't a pack. The two of us weren't a pack, that's impossible."

"I can't hear you anymore, Scarlet," he said. "I can't feel you in my mind, like your mother. You're just gone; you vanished. I thought you died for a moment. I'm weaker now. I'm weak. Now I'm just an ex-alpha."

"You were an ex-alpha ten years ago," I said quietly.

"But I could still hear you. I knew how you feel, where you were. Though now you're just... disconnected. That only happens when you leave a pack for another."

Everything was starting to get fuzzier. I rubbed my temples. "I didn't join a pack!" I yelled, giving myself a larger headache.

"Don't you get it?" my dad asks, pain on the edge of his voice. "Nathan is your family now."

I couldn't remember anything else. I couldn't see anything but the blurry world coming into what I call way-too-comfortable darkness.

Maybe

Scarlet falls to the hospital floor and we all call her name, yelling with worry. It seems as if her knees were knocked off beneath her. She steadies herself with her hands as she collapses, but soon her head hits the floor too.

It was definitely not a pretty sound to hear.

The last thing we heard escape from her mouth was a little yelp.

She was put in a room right next to her father's, which was really no surprise. Now Scarlet is sleeping, hopefully it's a peaceful sleep for her. She really needs it.

"She's going to be fine, right?" I heard Nathan say for the hundredth time.

"Yes, Mr. Adams," the doctor sighed again. It's not his fault though, I was tired of Nathan asking the same question every five minutes. "If you keep worrying, you'll end up on one of the beds yourself."

"Yeah, well..." For once, Nathan was out of words.

"Calm down for a bit, alright?" I heard the doctor say, and then his footsteps started to echo.

Nathan came back in the room, closing the white door behind him.

"How long are you going to keep asking that?" I ask with a smirk.

He rolled his eyes as he sat down in one of the comfy chairs. "I'm just... worried."

"And Scarlet is just tired," I shrugged.

"I made her tired though. I feel bad," Nathan frowns. "Is this really what happens when a werewolf bites another werewolf?"

My eyebrows furrow at the question. "Not particularly. Usually, when werewolves mate, it is through love bites, but it they don't really affect the other's... health."

"But why is she sick now?" he whispers, and the tension of the room had turn serious.

I looked straight at him. "Didn't you hear what Mr. Perez said? You and Scarlet are together now. New pack, new family. She left her dad's pack," I said, quoting the word. "She's completely with you now, all yours. Don't you see, Nathan? You are meant to be an Alpha."

"I'm not ready though," he sighs, running his hand through his hair. "I'm not ready to start a family, to take care of a whole pack. I'm seventeen for God's sake. We're too young."

I smiled. "There is no age limit to destiny, Nathan. And there never will be."

I needed the quietness in the room. Even with the solemn beat of the monitors, it was considered quiet to me. Scarlet's chest rises and falls, and I panic as it rises, because for some reason I always think it will be the last breath she takes. I'm not usually this much of a pessimist.

April had left to go home for the night, so I was alone. For the last minute I had sighed probably five times already, thinking about her words. *There is no age limit to destiny, Nathan. And there never will be.* Was she right? Am I meant to do this?

Am I meant to be an Alpha? To be Scarlet's mate? Or is this all just an odd dream that my scarred mind had scraped up? All I know is that I'm not ready.

Or am I?

We could go back to Canada - Scarlet and I. We can run in the woods without a care in the world, and maybe once in a while go to her grandparents' house for a feast. I can tell my mom how I've finally moved on with my life, and how I already have a family at such a young age. Would she be proud of me if she were here?

Is she looking down at me now?

Who would want to be in a pack with me anyways? I've only been a werewolf for a few days. I've only changed a few times in Canada. I'm inexperienced. So how am I meant to do this?

Sighing, I pull the chair I was sitting in over to the bed. I hold Scarlet's hand in mine, and I ask her quietly, "What do you want in our future, Scarlet?" I whisper in the quiet room.

I had already turn out the lights, since it was night and I was most likely staying over. The moon was the only thing lighting up the room, lighting up her face. It was so peaceful, even in the hospital. It felt like it was just Scarlet and me.

"Scarlet?" I whispered again. "Do you think I'm up for this?"

It was quiet until she replied.

Don't ask me... ask yourself. She said.

"I did," I respond. "I already asked myself."

No. Not your human-self. The werewolf in you. Ask him.

"How do I do that?" I questioned. She didn't answer. "Scar?"

My mind was completely blank, not a thought came to mind. I took in the silence with a sigh, and I watched Scarlet. Her red hair, her freckles... those long eyelashes, those soft lips of hers... And even though her eyes were closed, I could imagine her grey eyes, watching me carefully.

Within just months I have fallen in love with this girl. I really can't believe it. Is love supposed to be this rushed? Is this how mating works? Is it this fast? Or was this meant to go downhill, and end tragically? I'm just... I'm just scared that I'll mess up... that I'll kill my own family because of a stupid incident.

I don't want any of them to end like up like my mom.

And I sure as hell know that Scarlet doesn't want any of her relatives dead.

I rub my temples, trying to clear my head again. I think too much. If I keep doing this, I'll lose all of my hair before I'm even thirty years old. And for the slightest of a second, I imagined myself as a fur-less wolf.

What a funny yet sad picture to imagine..

Letting out one last breath, I kiss Scarlet's hand and before I knew it, I drifted off into a heavy sleep.

My hand was losing blood flow. How did I know? Well, for one, I couldn't feel it. And two, I couldn't move my fingers. And the last reason is that Nathan was practically sleeping on my hand.

What ever happened to pillows?

I move my hand out of his weight, and tried to get my blood to flow. After a few minutes, my hand was back alive, and I my eyes move to the little boy sleeping on the bed.

His lips were slightly parted, and his cheeks were flushed. His eyelashes were even longer than mine, and I was definitely jealous of his perfectly arched eyebrows. He looked really... adorable when sleeping. I couldn't resist though, I ran my fingers through his soft dark hair.

He didn't wake, which was good. As I run my fingers over and over through his hair, I began to think about last night.

Nathan had asked me what I wanted in our future - our. He wants a future with me. I was quite surprised that the monitors didn't show how oddly my heart had beat when he said that sentence, but I was happy nonetheless. But I can't help but ask myself, Do I really have a future with Nathan?

What will happen? Will we get married? Will others join our pack? What will happen to my dad? Will we have to move? Is he going to move in with me? Are we practically together already, or do I need a ring? When will we have kids? What will I do as a career? How will Nathan be as a father?

I don't know. I just don't know.

"Scarlet," Nathan's morning voice sent me shivers. "Ah," he said as he touched the hand that was massaging his head. "I'll never get tired of that."

I smiled. "How did you sleep?"

When he stretches I see his belly button... for such a simple thing, I blush. To my disappointment, Nathan sees me and smirked. "My back is killing me, but other than that... nothing was haunting me in my dreams."

My eyebrows furrowed. "Do you have nightmares at night, Nathan?"

He started to scratch the back of his neck. "Sometimes... it comes from time to time. They're usually about... my mom... the accident... those things..."

Without hesitation, I sit up to hug him.

"Why?" he asks simply.

"I know it hurts for you to be here, Nathan," I said quietly. "I can feel your pain right now. Don't forget that alright?"

He sighs and wraps his arms tightly around my waist.

"What are we going to do, Scarlet?" Nathan asks, breathing into my hair.

I pull out of our hug, and looking into his eyes. "We're going to... we're going to start out fresh. We're going to look for people who want to be in the pack, since you're now an Alpha and all," I said, smiling. "But we can't do any of this until school is over... okay? I just need to get one part of my life accomplished."

He nods. "Okay, I understand."

"Maybe after, we can start to have an actual family. And maybe even move to Canada. We'll have our own place... and it'll be just us. We're going to live happily ever after and... that'll be the end." I smile again, but he frowns.

"What if I screw up?" he whispers.

"Well then, Nathan," I said. "Maybe screw-ups are meant to be in your destiny. Maybe all of this... all that we've been through is your destiny. To run across the woods with fast speed... to hunt... to feel the adrenaline..."

I shake my head and stare into his forest-green eyes, eyes that I'll never get tired of.

"Or... Maybe we'll create our own destiny, together."

Milton Keynes UK
Ingram Content Group UK Ltd.
UKHW021429210923
429112UK00013B/576